Flood Tide

K N Boyle

Sequel to *The Random Killing*

1 From the Deep

Strait of Juan de Fuca
  Near Neah Bay, Washington
  Wednesday, August 17, 2011 1:05 AM PDT

"Torfino Weather station, this is the yacht John Watson checking in again."

"This is Torfino Weather Station, John Watson. What is your location and status?"

The wind pushed the next wave against the side of the forty foot yacht causing the captain to lurch sideways steadying himself against the side of the cabin, as he continually adjusted course.

He keyed the mike again. Even inside the yatch's pilothouse the thunder made the captain pause before responding, "Torfino, this is the John Watson, our location is 48.4 north, 124.7 west. We got the bilge pumps repaired and running again. We're running on fourth reef. Did not see Juan de Fuca buoys but GPS shows us within the strait now."

"Roger that John Watson, we will contact Port Angeles and give them your location. They will take over from here. Safe travels, Torfino out."

The John Watson continued to rush forward through the deep water of the strait ten miles from either Canadian or US shores. Pounding rain limited visibility. Lightning bolts lit up the twenty foot waves pushing them forward. They were close to safe anchorage, but exhaustion was draining them. The remaining ten miles of raging ocean meant survival was not guaranteed. They were the only boat on the strait, and feeling the loneliness

At 1:25 AM the door of the pilothouse slammed open. The first mate yelled above the wind and waves.

"Dad, mom, I saw breakers four points off port! About fifty yards off!"

The captain instinctively looked left and saw only the rain blown against the window.

"We're in the middle of the strait, Jim. There are no rocks for nine miles at least."

Jim unclipped his safety line from the rail and stepped into the pilothouse sliding the door shut, "I'm telling you Dad, I saw waves breaking off port."

The captain stared left again into the dark. A sudden flash showed a wave breaking against rock, but this time the rocks were only two points off port.

"Dad, did you see that? "

"Yeah. Either those rocks are moving forward or we're sailing backward! Jim, take the wheel. Janet, keep an eye on me."

The two switched places while the captain pulled the safety clips from his life jacket pockets. He opened the door to the pilothouse and immediately clipped his safety line to the outside rail. He slid sideways along the port side hanging onto the cabin. He saw his wife knocking on the window and pointing ahead. He looked up in time to see another flash of lightning strike the obstacle two hundred yard ahead of them. The captain waited for the next flash to help steady his nerves, but in the next flash the obstacle turned and the captain saw the face.

The captain's stomach churned as he stumbled back to the pilothouse. "Check the depth finder, Jim!" he barked through the open door.

"It reads one eighty five meters, more than six hundred feet."

2 Colossus

Sail River Inlet
  State Route 112
  Neah Bay, Washington
  Wednesday, August 17, 2011 after Midnight PDT

Tony McCarty was at least glad he wasn't in a boat in this weather as he pulled on his oil skin coat and foul weather gear. "Some people like going out in the storms," he complained out loud to no one in particular. Everyone else was sleeping in the back bedrooms and didn't hear.

Tony walked out the door into the gale. There was no bridge for the narrow stream called Sail River. He headed to the narrowest part of the stream where he could walk into the water and step over the deeper section. The inlet was well protected from pacific rollers pounding the outer beaches. Once across he walked along the inlet toward the opening to the deep water of the strait where he was exposed to the forty knot winds and spray from the breakers. He looked up and down the coast.

In the flash of lightning Tony saw something rolling in the surf. He expected to find his crazy father-in-law's body. He waited for a wave to break and then dashed down the rocky shore to grab the old man. He was relieved to find only a section of log covered in seaweed.

The next wave didn't crash and Tony felt something suddenly block the wind. He looked up and saw only blackness crushing down.

4

3 Normal Workload

FBI Offices, 23rd Floor
26 Federal Plaza, New York City
Thursday, August 18, 2011 8:45 AM EDT

Angela's personal affects had been given to her family after the funeral. Tommy now looked through the box of Angela's FBI equipment. He removed the stapler he found and put it on his desk, tossing his into the box.

Tommy walked down the hall to the White Collar Crime area, "Guys, this is Angela's stuff. Take anything you want."

"I'll take the stapler," Carlos said looking into the box.

Tommy said, "I already have the stapler. That one's mine."

"They're identical, how can you tell?"

"Just take what you want and put the rest back in the supply closet," Tommy said walking back.

Steve looked in and poked around. He found a chess knight underneath everything. He walked back to his desk and placed it in front of his computer screen. Carmen didn't want anything.

Tommy spent hours filing expense reports and damage assessments. His cost center was officially over budget for the month and still had two weeks left. The daily flood of action reports and information requests Tommy assigned to Carlos to coordinate with Steve and Carmen.

The disadvantages of becoming a media darling were becoming obvious. Tommy's tackle on the Random killer had the third most YouTube hits of all time when you added up all the sites showing it. Most of the sites ran the New York City footage parallel with Tommy's quarterback sack in the Syracuse game. Both tackles ended with a stretcher.

Tommy re-read the email from Mr. Rorbach, the Assistant Director for CIRG commending the entire Serial Events Task Force for the handling of the Random case. An ominous question at the end of the email asked, "Is it possible for Agent Haskins to have his facial tattoo removed?"

4 Start Investigating

"Kevin, All I'm asking is that you keep the nut cases out and block access to Sail River. You could start by towing all the campers parked on route 112. The Makah Days festival starts in one week. This is our biggest tribal culture day of the year. My own parents won't come if this mess isn't cleaned up!"

The sheriff seated behind his desk shook his head, "Pete, we've had cruisers out there every day since mid-August. We're getting killed by all the other cases we are supposed to be working on. It's your reservation. Use your people to police it."

Pete Sandro, tribal elder sporting a Red Sox ball cap said, "We can't handle the volume. There is a line of cars and RVs from Port Angeles trying to get to Sail River. And who is investigating the dead guy? Tony McCarty's widow is causing all kinds of trouble for the Makah tribe. Not to mention every UFO and Sasquatch hunter in the world is either here or on the way."

Sheriff Kevin Miller leaned forward, "Pete, what am I supposed to do? I can call the FBI office again. They're responsible for helping the reservations with stuff like this."

"Yes, only this time skip the Poulsbo office and call Seattle. The agent from Poulsbo left for some conference in Ohio."

Kevin got an idea and dialed a number saying, "Pete, I'll do you one better. Yes, Congressman Norm Dicks' office, please."

"Okay, may I speak with Sharon Ryan?"

-

"Ms. Ryan, this is Clallam County Sheriff Kevin Miller. The Makah tribe in Neah Bay needs FBI help with a murder on the Makah Reservation. It's the one in the tabloids."

-

"No, I'm only asking for your office to make some calls to get more attention from the FBI. You've seen the news. We can't handle a case this size. The Sheriff's office is helping the best we can but the traffic alone ..."

-

"You will? Thank you, that would be a big help."

-

The sheriff hung up saying, "Pete, I guarantee Norm's office will get something started but he will want you to pose for photos with him. Nothing's free."

Pete shot back, "I still need help with all the cars we have impounded and stop the traffic at the US 101 off-ramps at 112 and 113."

"Ahhh Pete, you're killing me! I can send tow trucks to remove all the vehicles you have and anything on the state route but the side streets are on you."

"What about the off-ramps?"

5 FBI Request

FBI Offices
  Abraham Lincoln Building
  1100 3rd Ave, Seattle, WA
  Tuesday, August 23, 2011

"Yes Ms. Ryan, we are working on the case. Agent Grimes was on site again yesterday with a forensics technician. We are processing the ... yes, I know this is hurting the lumber business. No Ma'am, I cannot send agents out to control traffic. Route 112 is a state highway. I can ask the sheriff ... huh, she hung up."

"That sounded serious."

Special Agent Rogers said, "That was Sharon Ryan, Congressman Norm Dicks' office manager. She is probably calling DC right now. Pull Hayworth off the Fusion Center assignment and send him out to the Makah reservation to coordinate the investigation. Better to be proactive when DC asks what we are doing about it."

6 Cambourne Hall

A Private Estate near Oxford, England
Friday, August 26, 2011 9:30 AM GMT (5:00 AM EDT)

Alicia said, "I believe you have some references for me."

The nattily dressed man sat bolt upright across the small desk from Alicia in the butler's pantry where Alicia was doing all her interviews. He handed her an envelope and said, "I was told the lady of the house would be interviewing me."

Out in the kitchen a board fell to the stone kitchen floor making a jarring sound.

The Scottish construction manager responded, ""Have a care there ya bloody oaf. This house is older than your whole family tree. And you, doan be putting your tool box on the counter. Have ya got no sense in ya at all, man."

Alicia turned her attention away from the ruckus outside the door and back to the gentleman sitting across the small desk from her, "I am the lady of the house," she said ignoring the condescension in his voice and viewing his list of references.

Alicia continued, "How large a staff did you manage at your last position?"

"You are a child and an American. I was told that ..."

"Lift the bloody thing inta place, doan just look at me," came from the kitchen around the corner from where Alicia and the prospective butler sat.

Alicia rose from her seat saying, "Just a minute please," and she walked out into the short hallway leading to the kitchen.

Alicia heard the eighth gentleman she had interviewed huff, "Of all the nerve!" under his breath.

Alicia watched the construction crew straining to lift the heavy stainless steel hood into place over the new commercial stove and grill top.

"Stan' back there Missy," the manager warned, followed by, "No, no, prop the edges up with the boards!"

Alicia picked up a ten foot long board at her feet and lifted it to prop up the nearest side of the hood that was sagging. She then pushed the bottom forward toward the stove to lift the hood higher.

"Oh, that's good." the manager shouted, "Jest a wee bit more."

Alicia kicked the bottom of her board and it moved another inch forward lifting the hood the bit more.

"Ah Missy, that's perfect. What a godsend you are. Bolt it in lads."

Alicia stepped forward to the Scotsman who was watching the bolts anchor the hood into place, "Excuse me, what is your name?"

"Name's Aindroo, Missy, Aindroo MacKenna. What can I do for you?"

"You were managing the rearrangement of the bedrooms yesterday and now you are supervising building improvements. This morning you were inspecting the grounds."

"Not tight enough there, Skippy. At least two more cranks on your ratchet," Aindroo directed followed by, "It sounds, Missy, that there is a question you'll be wanting to ask but I haven't heard it yet."

"Um, yes, what else do you do for the estate?"

"I am just here to get the estate prepared for his lordship's residence but is that any business o' yours?"

Alicia tried not to be intimidated by the man's massive presence and brusque manner. Without his wool cap his short gray hair and square head made him look even bigger. His thick calloused hands looked to be carved from oak with a sturdy stance and walk as if he expected to be collided with at any minute.

Alicia replied, "I am the lady of this manor, or I will be. You seem to know everything about this estate and I need help managing it. I don't know what I'm doing."

"Oh wale, you've cornered yourself a prize groom and in a hurry to marry him before he changes his mind. And you'll probably be pregnant no doubt. Of course you have no idea what you're doing."

Alicia took a deep breath and responded in a controlled manner, "Aindroo, in order to be pregnant there are certain, um, preliminary activities that I have not availed myself of. So to put your mind at ease, no, I am not pregnant."

"Wale, you're not pregnant and I am not a butler like that puffed up peacock sitting in the butler's pantry. He has the correct training and certification, certainly, but he no' has any manners. Took care of the dowager Hempstead until she passed, no trouble, but he pissed off every man jack in the shire to get his way and wasn't too keen on his mistress either. No, it wasn't for the mistress' sake. He's just an ass."

"You see," Alicia pleaded with her hands open, "that is exactly what I need, someone to tell me the truth, straight out. Someone who knows the people. Would you consider a position as the estate's manager?"

"I woan be serving you tea and cookies. You can forget that, and I'll want the staff to answer to me."

Alicia straightened, "I'm not asking you to be a butler, Aindroo."

Aindroo looked right at Alicia with a fixed gaze. Alicia did not flinch.

Finally he said, "Wale, okay then, you have yourself an estate manager but I am very expensive. And you can tell the peacock to run along home."

Alicia returned to the kitchen after dismissing the peacock. Aindroo was putting tools away. He spoke without looking up, "If I'm to work for you I need to make a few things clear."

"Yes?"

Aindroo stood and faced Alicia speaking clearly, "I'll work for you. Weel no' be friends. I woan be calling you Missy. You'll be called 'your ladyship' and one thing most clearly, you'll no' be making sport o' how I talk. None o' these are negotiable especially that last one."

Alicia nodded and said, "Aindroo, not another soul will ever catch me making sport o' how you talk. No' another soul."

Aindroo scowled but agreed, "No' another soul."

Alicia stuck out her hand.

"Your ladyship should no' be shaking hands with the help and my hands are filthy."

"I was raised mostly by my father on a potato farm in Ohio. The dirt on your hands is nothing compared to what I have worked in. Also, I am not your ladyship until we shake on it."

Aindroo shook her hand but added, "And that's another thing your ladyship, weel no' be talking about anything you did that a lady o' the manor house should no' be doing. No more discussing honest work that you and your father did. Now go wash your hands ... please, your ladyship."

Alicia looked at the dirt and grease on her hands as she walked towards the kitchen sink, "Dirty hands are a badge of hard work my father told me."

"It will be a badge o' dishonor for a lady, your ladyship."

7 Private Converse

Cambourne Hall
  Near Oxford, England
  Friday, August 26, 2011

"It sounds like a conspiracy."

"Nonsense Alan, you've missed the point by a continent. We are merely a group of Englishmen looking to secure Britain's future. I am surprised Mr. Clarke did not make this clear to you at the outset."

Alan and his guest walked past different work crews in search of a quiet space to talk. Alan directed, "I believe the morning room has been completed. Right through the long gallery here. We will take the door on the left."

A temporary office on the stone paved morning room overlooking the lawns and gardens stretching out behind the manor. Tall windows lit and warmed the room when the sun shone. Today low clouds hurrying by spoke of cooler weather on the way. The Scottish construction manager, who was in the kitchen, had built a fire in the hearth and set a sheet of plywood across saw horses as a work space for himself. Blue prints, notebooks and his computer were spread across the surface.

"Mr. Blackton, I apologize that I cannot offer you tea. We are just getting settled in. Mr. Clarke had promised to fill in more details but has been out-of-pocket these days."

"Quite all right, the tea I mean. Yes, quite busy these last weeks," Blackton said adding, "You know he has spent a considerable amount of political capital putting you in this position. I trust you will do your part. Also, I must say, you've made a bold move hiring MacKenna.

Completely untried at this sort of thing. You will need to take charge of the situation. Don't let him run off and start firing all the staff."

"I'm sure there won't be any need for that. We are trying to keep the house running smoothly, but what do you mean 'doing my part?'"

8 Cassanzo

Cassanzo Villa
  Near Orsara di Puglia, Province of Foggia, Italy
  Monday, September 5, 2011

"One flashing red light two kilometers distant will not keep you awake, father, and now we have power and cell phone coverage," Roberto explained.

"We don't need help from Señor Ciulli," the old man croaked from his bed. "Where is our money?"

Roberto turned back at the doorway, "Stefano is looking into the problem and you should thank Luigi Ciulli. Now my family and I can stay here with you."

Roberto walked into the great room hearing hoarse words followed by a racking cough. Agosto sat at one of the tables watching him come. The old vintner lifted his hand, "Hey Roberto, is it true, somebody stole all our money?"

"Not all of it but much of it. While we were worried about Sutton driving us out of business someone emptied several investment accounts. You told me when I was small, 'Vines don't grow by themselves. You have to watch them and help them grow.' Money is the same way. We were not allowed to watch it and it was stolen."

"You should get that enforcer, what was his name?"

"Salvatore. Yes, Stefano is trying to talk to him."

The leathery lines on Agosto's face broke into a big smile, "Teresa is back with Stefano. I knew she would come back. I always liked her."

9 The Help

Cambourne Hall
  Near Oxford, England
  Friday, August 26, 2011

"No, I won't have it. That's final."

"Alan, he had to do it."

"He had to fire all the staff? I don't believe that was necessary."

Workman watched the couple's first argument. Alan and Alicia walked into the library for privacy. "He didn't fire them all," Alicia quietly explained, "He kept the cook, upstairs maid, gardener, and motorman."

"Blackton warned me he might do something like this and now he's gone and done it. Well I want them all back this afternoon!"

Alicia smiled, "Alan dear, who is Blackton?"

"Why, he is the representative from Mr. Clarke, of course."

"Ah," Alicia said with growing understanding, "Dear, MacKenna fired the staff because they had not been hired. They just showed up to work here after William Sutton died. They had good credentials but they were all from London and nobody here knew them. MacKenna hired people he knew. My guess is that Blackton put them here to spy on us."

Alan said, "Unbelievable. Do you trust this MacKenna?"

"He's too annoying to be dishonest. He doesn't care what anyone thinks about him and he does know his business."

"So assuming he is the man for the job, are we up to full staff now?"

"According to MacKenna there were too many on staff. He fired eight and brought in three. The rest of the work he will hire out to local companies."

10 Wedding

Alicia took her father's strong arm while her attendant pulled her veil over Alicia's face. The three bridesmaids filed past them in measured step with the bridal march. Dale Montgomery, the potato farmer from Ohio, met his daughter's gaze. Tears flowed on both sides of the shared moment.

"Alice, this is a fairy tale wedding and you are the princess I always knew you were."

"I'm scared, Daddy. How did I get here? What do I do? What if I fail?"

Mr. Montgomery looked ahead to the groom and groomsmen waiting with the vicar on the raised dais at the end of the hall, "Honey, you got here one step at a time. Do you see that man waiting for you?"

"Yes Daddy."

"Ignore everything else; keep your eyes on him. Times will be hard. This will be the most difficult job you will ever take on. Together you and Alan will change the world we live in. Your life together will affect generations, reaching down the halls of time. Just keep your eyes on that man. Ignore his successes. Ignore his failures. Just focus on him."

Alicia's mind was swimming as her father's words opened unseen dimensions, showing her a place in history, a space in the world, and for the first time in her life she felt the waiting intimacy of shared lives. She would be completely vulnerable, naked in every respect to this man waiting for her.

"It's time, Alice."

"I'm ready, Daddy."

Macy Montgomery stood as her daughter stepped through the arch onto the white satin runner. All stood and watched.

"This actually is a fairy tale wedding," Cynthis Strath-Whitman whispered to her sister, "Here comes Cinderella."

Her sister sniffed, "And there are the three ogres, the father of the bride and his two brothers. All we need is a troll to make it complete"

Cynthis replied, "That would be the Scotsman in the kitchen."

11 Looking for Father Rand

New Hope Homeless Shelter
Sutter Avenue, East New York City
Saturday, September 24, 2011 7:10 PM EDT (12:10 AM GMT)

Nina missed the mood change. She was too busy directing men in the kitchen. Subtle at first, a lull in conversations, then feet started shifting, discussions began again, but this time with an edge of nervousness. Suddenly men who should be outside having their last smoke began walking back indoors looking nervously around. Nina now took note. The homeless, more sensitive and volatile to perceived threats, get dangerous quickly. She needed to head off trouble. Nina stepped into the dining room and the heavy metal door to the street burst open. A crazed addict ran in screaming, "He's here! The demon man is here! Hide me, protect me!"

Nina was struck dumb as the lone man raced through the kitchen and out the back door. Other men started moving away from the front door as Nina could feel a presence approaching. The air was alive with energy. The door started moving inward slowly causing each person in the dining room, Nina included, to move back and hold their breath.

A hand came around the corner of the door and Nina heard, "Hello, is it okay? Can I come in?"

Nina's mouth, which had been hanging open, snapped shut when a sandy haired visitor peeked in and then walked in the door wearing a blue button down shirt, khaki pants and nice loafers. Nina was about to laugh when several other men started screaming and ran out the back door.

"Is Father Rand here?" the stranger asked meekly.

Nina shook her head and returned to the open mouth posture.

The man saw Nina and looked sheepish, "Is Father Rand here? If not I can come back. I didn't mean to cause any trouble."

Nina shook her head again, "Uh, no, Father Rand is not here. Who are you? What's going on?"

"I am so sorry, my name is Andy Glover. I'm a friend of Father Rand."

"You? You're Andy Glover? You aren't supposed to be here. You are not allowed to be here. You need to leave."

"Father Rand said I could try stopping by on a Saturday evening just to give it a try. He's not here?"

A ruckus behind her caused the petite twenty four year old Nina to turn to the kitchen and yell, "Quiet down!"

The yelling did not quiet. She responded with a thunderous, "I said can it!"

Silence took over the main floor.

Turning to Andy, Nina said, "Father is not here right now. You should have called ahead."

"Sorry, I just came into town and needed to talk to him. Do you know when ..."

"Hey, I know you," Nina interrupted, "You're that guy on the news, the shooting, downtown Manhattan, and something about the Italian princess who died."

12 Reception

Cambourne Hall, Long Gallery
  Near Oxford, England
  Saturday, September 24, 2011

The wedding speeches finally over, the couple was able to sit and eat. Alan's second fork of prime rib arrived at his mouth along with the sensation of being watched. A sideways glance found his bride staring at him and smiling.

Alan returned the smile saying, "You are beautiful, my dear."

Alicia blushed turning away but then turned back to face Alan with fire in her eyes. Alan, caught off guard, leaned away from Alicia causing many to look at the couple uncertain of what happened. Alan watched Alicia's face change expression rapidly. Suddenly Alan pulled Alicia out of her seat spinning her onto his lap and leaned into a smothering kiss. Alicia pulled Alan down even harder.

A gasp rippled through the assembled guests followed by Alicia's parents and uncles applauding and Uncle Carter gave a whoop. The kiss lasted longer than expected and the Americans renewed their approval. Finally Alan lifted Alicia up and spun her back into her seat.

Cynthis Strath-Whitman's sister whispered, "Very unseemly."

Cynthis stared open mouthed and started fanning herself. After a pause she said, "Yes, quite. I think I'll take some air." She stood and walked out not waiting for her sister.

Macy approached a well-groomed Brit with an envelope held out in front of her, I believe this is from you." It was an accusation, not a question.

"Yes, Mrs. Montgomery. Mr. Harriman wished to express his best wishes to the new couple."

Macy tore the envelope in half saying, "Very cute. Tell Mr. Harriman this is my daughter not some janitor's third cousin. Send her some real estate. He has a nice little complex on Antigua, Indian Point I believe. That would be a more appropriate expression of his gratitude and good wishes." Macy stuffed the envelope pieces into the man's breast pocket.

With the official wedding tasks completed Alicia sat down abruptly in the back corner of the gallery. Aindroo watched over the festivities from the garden entrance He approached her, narrowing his piercing gaze, he said, "Your ladyship looks a might flushed and your forehead is perspiring. Do you have a fever?"

Alicia turned toward Aindroo with a panicked glare. Her scared look shook Aindroo. He was suddenly afraid for her.

"Aindroo," Alicia bit her lip and continued fanning herself, "I, uh, need to avail myself of certain preliminary activities ... now!"

Aindroo was confused until he remembered his first encounter with Alicia and relief flooded through him.

"Oh wale, not to worry, your ladyship," then turning to Gregor the butler he directed, "Go tell his lordship that he has an urgent communication. He can take it in the butler's pantry." A quick look back at Alicia and Aindroo corrected, "Tell him it is extremely urgent." Aindroo escorted Alicia out of the room.

Additional servants went in and out of the kitchen with desserts. Lord St. Claire came in with the flow calling out, "MacKenna, is there a call for me?"

Aindroo stood by the door to the butler's pantry and opened it without looking in, "Your lordship can take the call in here."

Alan walked into the pantry and Aindroo pulled the door shut. Then Aindroo walked into the kitchen to the sound of a loud thump against the adjoining wall in the kitchen.

A pastry chef was finishing the last trays of desserts. She looked up and asked, "What was that?"

Aindroo replied as he sat down with a cup of coffee, "That would be his lordship."

There was a muffled animal growl that caused two of the maid servants to stop and stare with open mouths.

Aindroo took a sip of his coffee and stated matter of factly from his seat, "That would be her ladyship. No discussing any of this or I'll see that none of you ever work again."

A sound like small beans falling on the ground caused Aindroo some confusion, but then he nodded. After another sip of coffee he said, "Moira, please set your tray down and get another dress shirt for his lordship. You'll find one hanging on the stand in his lordship's dressing room. Be quick, girl."

Moira fairly sprinted to the servant's stairs.

Mrs. Grady the cook looked stunned but said, "Maybe we should install a small couch in there."

Aindroo growled, "Weel no' be discussing this! Besides, we canno' very well put a couch in every room and closet on the estate."

Mrs. Grady went back to her pantry inventory sheet commenting, "This just might be a fun place to work again."

13 Father Rand

New Hope Homeless Shelter
   Sutter Avenue, East New York City
   Saturday, September 24, 2011 7:10 PM EDT

"I'm an adult. You can't tell me what to do!" Nina stated defiantly.

Father Rand turned away from her to face Andy, "You came here for help and I am advising you not to do this. She is a nun, well, almost a nun."

Andy's eyebrows raised and mouth dropped open.

Nina clenched her fists saying, "I have not taken my vows yet." Looking at Andy Nina explained, "I am a novitiate. I'm not a nun yet."

"Andy, as your friend I am asking you, don't do this."

"Look, I came here to talk," Andy said, "and get involved if I could, not to start a fight."

Nina's voice dropped into her mother superior tone, "That is not a problem. I am leaving now. Andy, you can come with me if you like, but I am leaving." Nina took her jacket off the rack. She walked out the front door through the crowd of people peaking in the door at Andy.

Father Rand buried his face in his scarred and tattooed hands. "Andy, you might as well go after her. She won't get two blocks in this neighborhood. Please hurry." Andy ran out the door scattering onlookers as they scrambled away from him.

Three men leaning on a car stood waiting for the nun to get closer.

"Nina, wait! I have a car."

The men saw Andy and started wandering off in different directions.

14 Dance Floor

Cambourne Hall, Long Gallery
  Near Oxford, England
  Saturday, September 24, 2011

One of the ogres approached the Strath-Whitman sisters. He bowed slightly and held out his sun browned, sinewy hand to Cynthis, "May I have the honor of a dance?"

Addyson, the elder of the middle-aged spinster sisters, replied, "Do all potato farmers know how to dance?"

Carter Montgomery answered, "I wouldn't know about that, ma'am. I'm a horse and cattle rancher."

Cynthis' face beamed suddenly and she took his hand. Rising, she said as she was led to the dance floor, "As a girl I wanted to be a show jumper. I was quite good."

Addyson frowned her disapproval.

Alan walked into the gallery smiling at the dancing partners and got his second shock of the night. One of the gossipy, busy body Strath-Whitman sisters was dancing a rumba with Alicia's Uncle Carter, who proved to be an exceptional dancer. To top that Cynthis was laughing and enjoying herself."

From behind a Scottish accent stated, "I wouldn'a believed it even if there were photographs."

Lord St. Claire asked, "Which, Cynthis or the farmer?"

MacKenna replied, "Either, your Lordship. Will you be dancing with her Ladyship? Should I ask the orchestra to play anything in particular?"

"At the moment her Ladyship is resting. When she is refreshed I think I could manage a decent waltz," St. Claire said. "What song is the orchestra playing? I like that."

"Very good, your Lordship. I believe the song is Paper Moon."

15 Café Gelato

Café Gelato
Greenwich Village
New York, NY
Saturday, September 24, 2011 8:50 PM EDT

"... and this elderly couple was watching TV when he dropped right through the ceiling into the middle of the room."

Nina gasped then laughed out loud.

"He could have gotten hurt. I wish I had been there to see the look on his face."

The night was pleasant enough to sit outside with their coffee. Other customers nearby enjoyed the warmth of their conversation, the laughter and lively stories. When Andy told about finding the stuffed bear in the box he got choked up and tears came to Nina's eyes. She wrapped her hands around Andy's.

Their discussion moved to other subjects and Nina kept holding hands prompting Andy to ask, "So, you're becoming a nun?" Nearby ears were shocked at the question.

Nina let go of Andy's hands and her voice dropped, "I decided not to take vows. I told Mother Superior. She asked me to give myself more time. She arranged with Father Rand for me to work in the shelter. That would give me exposure to typical work of our order. I told Father Rand what I had been thinking, and he tried to convince me to stay in the convent. I think that was why he was upset."

"It seems you have definitely made a decision to leave the convent. Shouldn't you be there now?"

"No, I've been staying with a family in Brooklyn. I need to let them know where I am, and that I have a ride home. Will you take me home?"

"Oh, of course."

16 FBI Request Again

FBI Headquarters
935 Pennsylvania Avenue, NW
Washington, D.C.
Tuesday, October 4, 2011

"Sharon Ryan from Congressman Norm Dick's office called again. She left me a message."

Deputy Director Tristano asked, "Yes Sir?"

"She says the next request will be from the Native American Political Action Committee straight to the White House. We need some high profile effort on this case. See that it is done."

Tristano pursed his lips then said, "Yes sir, I'll take care of it."

17 White Trash

Occupy Wall Street
Zuccotti Park, Financial District
New York City, New York
Wednesday, October 5, 2011 8:40 AM EDT

"*White trash or trailer trash was what most kids called me. Even after high school there was one boy I wouldn't date. He spray painted the words on my mom's front door and on my car. I have been fighting this feeling and reputation all my life ...*"

Steve looked around quickly and then back down.

"*... but you saw me. You looked at me and saw somebody special, not just a bartender with a pretty face. You didn't hit on me. You even noticed me working with Frank. He was the homeless guy sitting next to you. No one ever talked to me like you did. I wanted to know who you were, but you left. The owner was mad at me for taking a long break during the dinner rush, but I had to find you. I had to talk to you and then a miracle happened - you walked by.*"

Steve looked around again then back to his phone as the text continued,

"*I would prefer you didn't swear when we talk. It makes me feel bad. Please understand.*

Also, thanks to you I haven't had a cigarette in two weeks."

"Steve!"

"Sorry Tommy, did I miss anything?"

"I see you playing with your phone. Pay attention! The fuzzy hat guy is back in A2."

Steve sat up in his lawn chair inside Zuccoti Park and pulled the pirate skull cap down tight to make sure no one could see his ear piece. His facial tattoo was the perfect cover.

Carlos chimed in over the radio, "We have a positive ID on the lady with the baby stroller: Debra DeStefano, a database administrator from Verizon. Does anybody see her?"

"I assume she does not have any children with her," Tommy said scanning the park for a baby stroller from the second floor of Liberty One Plaza directly across from the park. "She probably has a laptop and one of the phantom WIFI hotspots in the baby carriage."

Carlos responded, "No record of any children."

Carmen broke in, "Carlos, the angry camo guy in 'D1' is accosting a business suit. No police are close. I'll call it in. Can you do a quick walk-by?"

"I'm on it," Carlos said as he stepped out of the delivery van parked on Cedar Street.

"Don't engage unless you have to," Tommy added.

"He's got a bulge in his belt under the vest," Steve called out with rising tension.

Carmen added, "He is unlikely to resort to violence. He threatens from a distance then slowly approaches as his victim shows fear."

They could all hear faint echoes of street chatter from Carlos' ear piece while they watched and waited.

"Carlos, turn around," Carmen said evenly, "There's another one of those kids. He just came out of Panini's right behind you. Dark brown hoodie with a backpack."

Carlos responded, "Okay, the suit is walking away. Direct me to the hoodie."

"Go back to G1 and look right. Steve, walk toward G2."

An annoyed Steve asked as he stood and started walking, "Carmen, why do you think this kid is a threat?"

"He doesn't fit the Occupy Wall Street profile but he does fit in with 'Invade Wall Street', early twenties tech geek, not engaged with the protest. He has his hood up and his head down. He's hiding even from the people in the park."

Steve said in an audible whisper, "I'm turning back. I'll approach from the Liberty Street side. Brown hoodie is sitting with the light blue hoodie kid and a male, mid-thirties, six foot even, about one ninety pounds, faded denim jacket."

"Why the re-direct, Steve?" Tommy asked.

"The group has two watchers. I don't mind them seeing me. I just want to make sure I catch the kids' faces when I walk by."

Steve walked slowly up the grid system Tommy's team used to identify areas in the park. Steve walked from H4 to G4 trying to look nonchalant, talking to people as he walked by them. When he got to F4 he looked right and saw both of the watchers eyeing him.

"Change of plan," Steve said.

Tommy watched as Steve turned right and walked toward the guarded group.

Steve called out, "You guys look suspicious as hell. What are you planning? Does the committee know about this?"

Steve looked directly at the denim jacket guy and the other watcher, then down at the kids. Light blue hoodie looked down. The kid in the brown hoodie looked up. He had bright red hair and an intelligent face. He also had an open laptop. He did not show fear but looked like he wanted to explain himself.

One of the watchers stepped forward menacingly, "Mind your own business. Keep walking."

Steve caught a faint eastern European accent.

Denim jacket spoke up reassuringly, "The committee knows about us. We are putting some flyers together for them."

"Then you don't mind if I ask them about you?" Steve countered.

"Not at all," denim jacket replied, "Tell them you spoke with Maury Ravel."

"I'll just do that," Steve said defiantly.

Steve frowned and took one more look at the hoodie kids and the watchers as denim jacket smiled unconvincingly. Steve turned and walked quickly toward the Broadway end of the park.

Steve talked as he walked, "If they are legit they will stay put while I talk to the committee. If not they will leave in different directions."

Carlos had returned to the van on Cedar, "I've got eyes on them, Steve. They're huddled up again. One watcher is following you at a distance."

Carmen asked, "Since the committee isn't here today who are you going to ask?"

"Him," Steve answered.

A man giving speeches from the top of the steps still had a crowd around him. Steve pushed through the small crowd to the speaker.

Steve said to the speaker, "Hey, we have a problem. There are some undercover cops in the park over there."

The watchers and the denim jacket guy saw Steve talking and then turn and point right at them.

Carlos said, "There they go. They're on the move."

"Which way did the light blue hoodie go?" Steve asked oblivious to the questions the speaker was asking him. No one in the crowd around Steve knew who he was referring to. They looked around for a light blue hoodie.

Carlos answered in Steve's earpiece, "He is in H3 and heading for the corner of Trinity and Liberty. It looks like he is heading up Liberty."

Steve said to the speaker and the crowd around him, "Never mind, I see them leaving now."

The watcher with the accent walked across Liberty Street and stood watching the light blue hoodie walk away. Then he turned and looked at Steve.

"I can follow light blue," Carlos said preparing to step out of the van.

Steve tensed as he saw in his mind's eye the positions of the visible players and probable positions of others.

"Stop Carlos!" Steve called out, "Stay in the van. Drive away, now! I'm coming toward you."

Carlos complied as Steve started running through the park toward Cedar Street. Steve cleared the park and saw denim jacket guy and the other watcher standing where the white van had been parked. They started following the van on foot but stopped when they saw Steve.

"Carlos, two of them were almost on you before you moved. That was close," Steve said while watching the two men turn back toward Trinity Place and then go in different directions.

18 FBI Offices

23rd Floor, 26 Federal Plaza
 White Collar Crime Division
 New York City, New York
 Wednesday, October 5, 2011 3:45 PM EDT

Scott LePage drew a line on the white board from a rectangle labeled 'Zuccotti Park' to another rectangle labeled 'Invade Wall Street'. Scott turned to face the group assembled which included Tommy's team and the CIRG section chief, Nathaniel Rorbach.

"You all know about the 'Occupy Wall Street' demonstrations going on in many cities, Scott started, "but now a group of loosely affiliated and socially conscious computer hackers known by the name of Anonymous have threatened to shut down financial institutions. They call their project 'Invade Wall Street.' Five days ago an unknown representative of Anonymous posted a threat to carry out their attack. Even though some in the group guessed the threat was bogus, the FBI and Homeland Security are required to take the threat seriously.

We had credible evidence some members of Anonymous would be among the demonstrators at Zuccotti Park, in the Financial District. Tommy Edwards' team from the Serial Events Task Force were staking out the park this morning. They were able to identify five potential members of Anonymous."

"Make that six," Steve Haskins corrected pointing at the board.

"Who are we missing?" Carlos asked.

"Angry camo guy," Steve responded, "I had to look at the surveillance videos to see it. He caused scenes all around the park loudly threatening people whenever police weren't around. He was fishing for undercover law enforcement. At 9:20 today angry camo guy started screaming at a passerby. That brought you out of the van walking toward him. That also gave the brown hoodie a chance to enter the park behind you. It was a coordinated set up."

"Did you arrest any of them?" a sharply dressed man called out as he walked quickly into the open office space of the white collar team. "You were looking right at them. Please tell me you arrested at least one of them."

CIRG chief Rorbach turned towards the late comer, "You must be Adams from Homeland Security."

The sharp suit snapped, "Yes I am and I want to know why you started this meeting without me?"

Rorbach turned away replying, "You're eighteen minutes late. You can read the minutes of the meeting to find out what you missed, and we don't arrest people for sitting in parks or walking on sidewalks. There was no probable cause for an arrest. LePage, continue with your meeting."

Despite grumblings from Adams, Scott LePage put up a photo of the brown hoodie guy with red hair.

"This photo was taken from Agent Haskins hat camera. You are looking at Larry Mastowski, database guru from West Virginia. If you think he has a baby face it's because he is twenty years old. Larry has no record. He is self-educated, highly self-educated in database platforms and programming."

Adams raised a hand asking, "If he has no education what makes him a highly educated guru?"

Scott said, "Let me put it to you this way, Larry sent Microsoft a list of corrections to one of their database manuals. Microsoft made the corrections in their next version. Larry was in eighth grade at the time. He also gave them his standard configurations for minimizing two ODBC scenarios that they had left out of their manuals. His versions have become industry standards for databases on virtual servers."

"Do you expect me to understand any of that?" Adams replied in a snobbish tone.

Scott smiled, "No, just so you know that Larry does."

Scott continued, "Larry was a guest speaker at COMDEX and CeBIT when he was a junior in high school, the two largest computer technology tradeshows in the world, COMDEX in the United States and CeBIT in Germany."

Scott LePage pointed back to the Invade Wall Street white board, "Critics of the Invade Wall Street October second announcement argued no single computer virus could take down all the different databases used by Wall Street financial firms. If it can be done Larry Mastowski will know how to do it or at least be a key player in it."

Carlos raised his hand, "Do we know Larry's whereabouts?"

"Not yet."

Rorbach asked, "Were any of the suspects armed?"

Carmen answered, "We saw no evidence of weapons but their expressions and actions show that they are not afraid of violence, starting it or responding to it."

"Also," Steve said, "Their movements were precise, tactical. I wouldn't be surprised if they had spotters and snipers in place."

Carmen noticed Rorbach grit his teeth each time Steve spoke, a classic sign of concealed disgust.

Each group represented in the meeting had follow up tasks, but Tommy's surveillance task was taken away by the CIRG chief. As the meeting broke up Rorbach called Tommy over.

"Tommy, I know we've had disagreements with staff and budgets but I need to ask a favor that won't make it any smoother between us."

"Is this about how you just pulled the rug out from under us just now?" Tommy said pointedly.

"Something like that. Tommy, I need your team to take over a politically hot investigation. You will have the lead on this case exclusively. You've heard of the Seattle sea monster?"

19 Team Huddle

"Carlos, close the door."

Carlos commented, "If Andy and Angela were here this would be very cozy."

"Okay, you all heard," Tommy began. "A CIRG unit will be taking over the surveillance for invade Wall Street."

"Is this because we didn't arrest anyone?" Carmen asked.

"No, we are being re-directed to take over a high profile case with a lot of political pressure. We will be flying to Seattle tomorrow to investigate a death associated with the Seattle sea monster."

Carlos rose from his seat, "Are you kidding? Tell me you're lying, Tommy."

"This is shit!" Carmen stated. "We have earned this case! Steve, say something. Don't just sit there!"

Steve sat with a stunned look on his face until Carmen called his name again.

"Uh, when do we leave?"

"What? Steve, is that all you have to say?" Carlos said.

Tommy narrowed his eyes at Steve, "What's with you? I thought something was different. You didn't swear and you look calm."

Steve truthfully responded, "I may look calm, but I don't feel calm at all if that helps. Now that I think about it, Tommy, you were always after me to be more professional, and stop swearing. So now you're mad because I missed a few opportunities?"

"Something is going on with you," Tommy said, "I know it. Also, you might as well know, I didn't put up a fight on the re-assignment because I need you out of this office for a while. I'm getting pressure about your face tattoo. What did you find out?"

"The doc told me the laser process won't work on the creases of the hammer lines so all they can do is take off some of the design. There is always the option of cutting off parts of my face and re-growing the skin, but you can forget that."

Tommy sighed and said, "Okay team, get out your travel bags. We are flying United. Meet in front of concourse A at 10:00 AM. Security will be waiting to walk us in."

20 LaGuardia

23rd Floor, 26 Federal Plaza
Tommy's Office
New York City, New York
Thursday, October 6, 2011 9:48 AM EDT

Carlos exited the cab and walked to the small group talking with airport security.

"This is agent Carlos Barrera," Tommy said handing Carlos his boarding pass. "We are missing one more. Here he is."

Steve walked up and Tommy said, "We have a change of plans, Steve. TSA officer Alvarez will take you over to concourse C. You are flying to San Francisco on US Air. I got a call this morning that Larry Mastowski is working in Silicon Valley. The company has been contacted and is expecting you."

"But then I meet you in Seattle, right?"

"Yes."

Carlos said, "Since we are looking for a sea monster should we call Andy? Won't cost the taxpayers anything."

"No," Tommy frowned, "We focus on our job."

Steve took a newspaper out from under his arm and smirked while handing it to Carmen, "There is a very good recap of the sea monster events on page four."

Carmen opened the paper as Steve walked away. The front page headline said, "Latest New York Billionaire Caught in Steamy Rendezvous with Nun."

The photo showed a nun's habit photo shopped onto a pretty girl holding Andy's hands while the two of them leaned in close.

The next line read, "Nun pleads, 'Take me home with you!'"

"Haskins, you asshole!" Carmen called out.

Steve turned around and yelled back, "Potty mouth!"

21 Unexpected Rendezvous

Marine Parkway
Redwood City, California, Silicon Valley
Friday, October 7, 2011 6:45 AM PDT (9:45 AM EDT)

"I do apologize, Agent Haskins, but building entry records show he usually is here by six."

"Thanks," Steve answered, "I'll keep watching from over there."

Steve returned to his observation spot peering through the ten foot floral arrangement watching for Larry to enter through the botanical garden the company built into their monstrous lobby. Inhabitants of the company flowed in and out of the doors in what appeared to be a contest to look more bizarre than anyone else and ride or skate on something no one else had.

Ten minutes later Steve's cell rang, "Haskins. Where? I'm on my way."

Haskins drove around the corner to the Sea Link Café. He spotted Larry's car immediately because of the yellow caution tape and police cruisers. He also noticed blood spray on the passenger window.

Steve walked through a small group of gawkers and showed his ID. He heard a gasp from someone in the crowd as an officer directed Steve to the detective. Steve stepped aside to take a call.

"Haskins," Steve said turning toward the café moving his head slowly sideways as the camera on his cell recorded the faces in the crowd. "I can't talk right now. I'll call you later," he said hanging up on the fictitious call.

"As you can see Agent Haskins, two bullets through the driver's window, head then chest. What can you tell us about Larry Mastowski?"

***

Later Steve pulled out his cell as he sat in San Francisco airport, "Tommy, that database kid, Larry Mastowski, was killed this morning in a coffee shop parking lot. Two shots through his car window, definitely an execution. It looks like he was waiting to meet someone. There were two coffee cups in his car. Hang on a second, Tommy."

A familiar feeling nagged at Steve while looking down at his phone. He turned on the camera again as he resumed the call, "I'm at the airport now. My flight is scheduled to land at SeaTac airport in two hours." Steve stood looking up at the list of departures while his camera scanned the terminal to his left. He then switched his cell the other ear and scanned to his right.

"One of the air marshals is meeting me any second.

-

"Okay, I'll meet you at the offices on Third Avenue."

22 Wedding Presence

Cambourne Hall, Drawing Room
Near Oxford, England
Friday, October 8, 2011 7:20 PM GMT (2:20 PM EDT)

Alicia opened the next box from the imposing wall of gifts stacked at the end of the drawing room.

Alicia read from the card, "Mr. and Mrs. Grant Wisener, South African Steel, all white china soup tureen, very nice."

Moira, the maidservant, set the tureen on the table with the other houseware destined for either the plate safe or the server room. Mrs. Hodson, the housekeeper wrote down name and gift on her notepad. Gregor, the butler, oversaw the evening's event while Alicia's mother talked on her cell phone pacing between the long gallery and the drawing room.

Moira said, "It wouldn't hurt anyone to let her join us. It might even make us a friend."

Mrs. Hodson gave Moira a hard stare.

"Well it wouldn't, now. She's harmless. It's her sister what's the mean one," Moira answered back.

Mrs. Hodson, determined to keep the conversation civil, returned, "That is not a proper conversation for this evening."

"Quite right," Gregor agreed while handing Alicia the next box.

Alicia read from the card, "From your friends and team mates, Tommy, Steve, Carlos, Carmen, Andy, and Angela (in absentia). It's a picture and ... a dark blue t-shirt."

Alicia handed the framed photo to Alan. The photo showed members of Tommy's group standing in front of the fountain in Foley

Square holding a portrait of Angela. They all wore dark blue t-shirts with bright yellow lettering, 'FBI - Serial Events Task Force'.

Alicia held up her t-shirt with the same lettering, emotion filling her eyes.

Alan explained to the staff, "This was the location of the shooting you have no doubt heard of. The portrait is of the woman Lady St. Claire tried to save. The FBI made her an honorary member."

"That's my girl," Macy stated proudly from the doorway. The staff were stunned and not sure what to think about the lady of the house. Apparently the news stories were true.

Alicia wiped her tears saying, "I can't believe they did this." She sighed and asked for the next box, and started unwrapping

Moira spoke up, "See, that is something the village would know about if she were here."

"Moira, stop or you will be sent out! That is not proper," Gregor said.

Alicia halted unwrapping the box listening.

Mrs. Grady, the cook, joined in, "What's not proper? They had tea and a walk in broad daylight. Some have nothing better to talk about."

Macy walked back to the group and sat.

Alicia asked, "Moira, who are you talking about?"

Gregor protested, "I have to agree with Mrs. Hodson, we have things to take care of and this is not appropriate."

Alan jumped in, "Gregor, what is this fuss about?"

Mrs. Grady answered, "Miss Cynthis, Sir. She had asked about coming over for a visit - without her sister."

"That is surprising, but what is the harm?" Alan asked.

Everyone else went silent so Mrs. Grady answered, "Miss Cynthis danced with her ladyship's uncle at the reception for quite a while."

"That was Carter?" Macy asked.

"Yes, Mum. The uncle decided to stay two extra days after your daughter left for the honeymoon. Sunday he was up early walking about the grounds and along the river. Monday he walked into the village and ran into Miss Cynthis. They had tea together and then went for a walk. That was all!" Grady emphasized her last point to Gregor.

Alicia asked, "So why is that a problem?"

Moira added, "Some people got their nose out of joint because Addyson had gone to London for the day leaving Cynthis and the cowboy alone and they took tea for two hours before the walk."

"They also stopped back at Miss Cynthis' cottage for another hour," Hodson said. "She said they were looking at horse photos but everyone is talking."

Macy threw in, "Big towns, small towns they're all the same. Gossip is the only excitement around and everyone likes a juicy story."

Alicia said, "At least daddy behaved himself."

Macy answered, "Nope, I caught him and that Scottish guy arm wrestling in the gun room."

Alicia said, "Okay, it could have been worse. Arm wrestling isn't a crime, but as far as Uncle Carter is concerned, let's invite Cynthis and her sister to dinner next week. Let her know that we aren't talking about her."

Macy commented, "It's not like she'll get pregnant."

"Mother!"

23 Get Out

FBI Offices
Abraham Lincoln Building
1100 3rd Ave, Seattle, WA
Friday, October 7, 2011 2:30 PM PDT (5:30 PM EDT)

Steve stepped out of the elevator into the main lobby. A tall thin blonde was giving instructions to Tommy, Carmen, and Carlos. The woman did a double take when she saw Steve approaching.

Tommy turned to look and introduced, "Sharon Ryan, this is agent Steve Haskins, the last member of our team.

Ms. Ryan looked intensely at Steve then said, "I don't remember you in the Foley Square videos."

"If you saw the video that showed the creepy thing disappear I was prone behind the fountain."

"As I recall you didn't fire at the shooter."

"Four shots as soon as they appeared, ma'am. After that people were running everywhere, no clear shot."

"Excellent discipline. My father was military police in Saigon. I understand the situation. When you come back to Seattle we should get together. I would like to get your view of what really happened."

Ms. Ryan cut off any response from Steve by turning back to Tommy, "Agent Edwards, as I said we need your presence on the ground in Neah Bay. Make sure you contact the yacht captain. Those are his monster pictures in the papers."

Tommy nodded, "We will get right out there, Ms. Ryan."

Sharon Ryan excused herself and walked quickly to the elevators.

Carmen smirked, "So tough guy, when will you be back in Seattle? Apparently Ms. Ryan likes your tattoo."

Steve ignored the comment and said, "Tommy, we should get moving. The traffic leaving the city on Friday is bad. We need to get to the Bainbridge Island ferry. I recommend we stop in Port Angeles for the night.

24 Port Angeles

The Gastropub
Port Angeles, Washington
Friday, October 7, 2011, 6:25 PM PDT (9:25 PM EDT)

Tommy and team checked into one of the cheaper hotels on the edge of town and drove into Port Angeles for dinner at a pub Steve recommended.

The crowd was noisy and well out of the pub and spilling over the sidewalk into the street in small groups. Steve sighed as the team walked closer to the packed burger bar. Nothing was going as he wanted; Sandy must have had her phone turned off, the database kid was dead, the Red Lion Hotel had no rooms, the streets and restaurants were full because of Crab Fest - not the homecoming he had in mind.

Carmen pointed out, "You said it was a good pub. The crowd agrees with you."

"Hey Steve, if you have any strings you can pull now would be a great time," Carlos said, "I'm tired. I just want to sit down."

Steve responded, "Let me at least ask if we can sit somewhere." Steve began wading through the crowd while the team watched.

Carmen laughed, "Hey, look at that sign! 'The newest brew – Blue Face IPA'. I am going to buy one for Steve."

As she completed her sentence someone shouted, "Blue Face!" Others noticed Steve walking by and started chanting, Blue Face, Blue Face ..." Tommy tensed, fearing he would need to drag Steve out before he started trashing customers. He took the first steps into the crowd and froze as a stunning blond walked around the bar and close up to Steve. Tommy, Carmen, and Carlos were paralyzed and then blown back as the bartender wrapped her arms around Steve's neck and kissed him passionately. The crowd went crazy shouting, "Blue Face," whistling and hooting. Steve had his arms around the bartender's waist, leaning into the moment. The kiss and the crowd kept on while Tommy and the team got more confused.

25 Business Meeting

Cambourne Hall, Gentlemen's Room
   Near Oxford, England
   Friday, October 7, 2011 3:20 PM GMT

"Good morning, Sir. Thank you for seeing me on such short notice," the well-dressed Italian said as he shook Alan's hand.

"Please sit," Alan offered. May I offer you coffee or tea?"

"No grazie, I won't take more than a few moments of your time. I am here for a client of mine who would request a favor."

"Forgive me but, who are you and who is your client?"

"Of course, my name is Salvatore. I am representing la familia Cassanzo. They had many dealings with the Lord St. Claire, previous."

"Salvatore?" Alan laughed, "With a single name you must be a rock star or a terrorist."

"I assure you, I am neither. Our previous dealings with Mr. Sutton left our relationship out of balance in your favor. I am here to request a favor to again bring balance to the relationship."

"See here, if you are trying to collect on a bill," Alan said sitting straighter, "you needn't have bothered coming here. You will need to contact our business offices in London. I can give you an address."

Salvatore's tone grew cold, "That is not why I am here. I will speak clearly. You owe a debt to Cassanzo. A simple favor is what I am asking."

Alan's terse response was delayed by Mrs. Hodson entering the room with a tray of coffee and cups, "Excuse me gentlemen, I'll be back shortly with tea and cakes,"

"That is not required, Mrs. Hodson ...," but Alan was cut short again.

"Good afternoon, I apologize for the intrusion."

Both men stood as Alicia entered. Alan said, "Dear, this is Mr. Salvatore. I am afraid he was just about to leave."

"That is not how we treat our guests," Alicia responded and held her hand out to Salvatore. "I am Lady St. Claire."

"Ah yes, the secretary," Salvatore said then kissed her hand.

"Are you trying to insult me, Sir?" Alicia scowled but did not withdraw her hand.

"In England it is an insult but in America and other places it is a great honor to rise above the position you were born into. In Italy you would be called bella, graziosa, una donna di valore."

Alicia sat next to Alan saying, "Thank you, Salvatore. You are very generous but tell us about where you live. I have never been to Italy. Have you, Alan?"

After Salvatore's brief description of his home on a large lake north of Rome along with some suggestions for the couple should they visit.

Alicia said, "Salvatore, you have been generous with your time and compliments, and I have no doubt that you will provide us with excellent travel arrangements when we visit, now how may we be generous to you?"

"As I was telling your husband, familia Cassanzo would ask a favor," Salvatore said. "There has been money stolen from this very good family."

"Please, tell us what you need," Alicia said.

"Familia Cassanzo was in a war with Lord St. Claire previous, William Sutton. While no one was watching someone made many stock purchases with Cassanzo money but the stock did not come to Cassanzo accounts."

"Where did it go," Alan asked.

"I have not been able to find the answer to that question though I have asked. Many people who managed these accounts and stock purchases were unfortunately killed. I cannot take this to law enforcement or government people in America, but that is who can find the answer. I am asking you to help my client avoid financial ruin."

Alan leaned forward, "This is the family of Celestina. I thought Cassanzo sounded familiar."

Salvatore said, "Yes, this family has suffered many sorrows. For now, the creditors will not press the family, but the time it is running out. I have been looking into this for over a month, every purchase traced is always a dead end. I ask that you talk to the FBI, the Congress, the courts, help la familia Cassanzo find their money."

Alan answered, "Signore Salvatore, if you are asking me and my wife to make introductions for you or ask people to get involved we would be happy to do that. If you are suggesting in any way that we would be responsible for the outcome, whether the Cassanzo's are able to recover their money, we will not agree."

"I need assurance," Salvatore said pointing at Alan, "That you will do all that is in your power to help the Cassanzos."

Alan quickly replied, "This is your responsibility not ours. We sympathize and are willing to get involved, but they are your clients." Alan continued as Alicia stared at him impressed, "We desire to bring balance, as you said, to this relationship with the Cassanzo family. I personally want to restore honor to this house, but as I stated we cannot guarantee success nor can we rightfully be held accountable for failure. You will need to represent the family to the American authorities or if you cannot someone from the Cassanzo family will need to represent them, someone in authority."

Salvatore leaned forward in his chair, "Yes, I will have one of the family get in touch with you, but he will get your full assistance. This home, this fortune, and name you have inherited, these have done great harm to Cassanzos. Your full assistance will be expected."

Alan said, "We will give every assistance, but the Cassanzos will need to do the work. We will open the doors; they will need to walk through them. I also need to know what resources you have to offer to resolve this situation. You cannot make demands and simply walk away. It just isn't done."

"I have many resources but also some limitations. I assure you I will be involved."

Alan stood concluding the meeting, "We need some level of detail to get the attention of the proper authorities. The person you select must be able to represent the family. Have them contact me with all possible information."

Salvatore nodded while rising, "They will be in touch. Lady St. Claire, are you ill? Your face is suddenly red and perspiring."

Alicia spoke with effort, "Alan, I'm feeling faint. Can you help me upstairs? Gregor can see Salvatore out."

26 Run Away

New Hope Homeless Shelter
Sutter Avenue, East New York City
Friday, October 7, 2011, 12:15 PM EDT

"She's run away, Andy. She's scared and can't go home or to the convent.
The press has been vicious, even here! They don't stop their cars, but
the drive bys never end. They constantly give the addicts money for
information. Our meal count is dropping and I know some will OD
with all the cash around."

"What can I do Father?"

"If I tell you where she is will you get her away? Hide her where
she's safe but, not alone, and not in any compromising situation, some
place safe."

"I could ..."

"I called a couple of convents but they would not shelter her. They
can't."

"Father Rand, I can ..."

"Can I trust you to keep her, you know, safe? I'm sorry Andy. I live
in a fallen world and just want her to be ... safe."

"Father, I can get her out of the city. I could have her call you every
day. Will that help?"

"I just want her to be safe."

"Yeah, you said."

27 In and Out

The Gastropub
    Port Angeles, Washington
    Friday, October 7, 2011, 7:35 PM PDT (10:35 PM EDT)

"Sandy, this is Tommy Edwards, my boss. This is Carmen and Carlos."

"Nice to meet you," Tommy said.

A confused Carmen asked, "How long have you known each other?"

Before Steve could answer a uniformed officer stepped up to the table, "Excuse me, Tommy Edwards? Clallam County Sheriff, name's Kevin Miller. Can we talk outside?"

Tommy excused himself and followed Sheriff Miller out.

All eyes at the table followed them out. As soon as they cleared the exit Carmen turned back to the table, "Steve, it's none of my business. I withdraw the question."

Sandy answered, "We met on August ninth, and we've been talking every day since then."

Steve responded to Carmen's disbelieving look, "I came here for my conditioning requirement. I met Sandy on the last day."

Sandy said, "He was the first guy in a long time who noticed me not just how I look. I was impressed."

"Oh really!" Carmen said with a smug grin and Carlos snickered.

Steve rolled his eyes and said, "Sandy, don't tell them anything. They'll only use it against me."

Tommy walked up quickly, "We need to go. There's been another incident."

Steve pulled a fifty out and handed it to Sandy, "This is for our food. Save my burger for me. You can give the other orders away." Steve squeezed Sandy's hand and walked out.

On the sidewalk the Sheriff gave the group a quick overview, "A sixty foot yacht was pulled under water by an unknown force. The yacht popped back up but several crew and the captain are missing, presumed dead. Two other boats nearby witnessed the accident. This happened a mile northwest of Neah Bay. A Coast Guard cutter is in route. You are needed on site as soon as possible."

"I assume driving is the quickest way there," Tommy said.

"It's all we have," Sheriff Miller said.

Tommy tossed the keys to Steve, "You drive. I'll ride with Sheriff Miller."

The Sherrif said, "Didn't you play for Penn State?"

28 Sound Advise

Wildcat Vista Road
    Snowmass Village, Colorado
    Friday, October 7, 2011, 9:50 PM MDT

"Andy, I can loan you the transportation. Just take good care of it and bring it back with a full tank of gas," Joe Harriman said, "You should bring her to Aspen. It's gorgeous here and there's celebrities under every rock. She won't be noticed."

-

"You're very welcome. I'm glad I can help."

-

"No, no, don't mention it. Your gratitude is payment enough. You'd be surprised how many people you try to help that actually turn and stab you in the back. They lie to your face and slam the door on you."

-

"I know you would never do that, Andy. I will warn you though, stay away from Lord St. Claire and his wife, Alicia. The British titles went straight to their heads, very ungrateful, no loyalty."

-

"Well, bring her to Aspen and you can all relax here. The leaves are turning and the mountain sides are golden."

-

"Okay, see you soon."

29 Warm House Restaurant

Makah Indian Reservation
  Neah Bay, Washington
  Friday, October 7, 2011, 11:55 PM PDT (2:55 AM EDT, Saturday
October 8)

"Don Hayworth," Tommy called out.

The restaurant was closed but almost every seat was occupied. Deputy Sheriffs, tribal police, tribal council members, witnesses, and well connected busy bodies made a steady drone of conversation. An older FBI agent looked up from the laptop and laughed when he saw Tommy walking through the door of the Warm House Restaurant. "Thomas Edwards, you sure took the long road getting here."

Sheriff Miller said, "The foot traffic on the road was unbelievable all the way here."

Carmen, Steve, and Carlos walked up and Tommy introduced the older agent, "Team, this is special agent Don Hayworth. He and I found the first evidence of the Random Killer."

"When I said long road I meant the road through Chicago, D.C., Philly, and New York," Don said rising and shaking Tommy's hand, "but I heard you are here to relieve me from this nightmare. Good timing too. The survivors of the crew docked in the marina a few minutes ago."

"You can't leave us just yet. Give us the rundown of today. Tomorrow we can discuss the rest of the case. "

"Coast Guard is towing the yacht back to Port Angeles. It has the nearest shipyard. Two of the three victims have been recovered. They are still searching for the captain. The bodies will be brought here tonight. Our forensics guy is Mark Ohashi. He's not on site yet. He's been added to your team for as long as you need him. I've been asking for forensic help for a month and couldn't even get a pair of tweezers. You guys show up and get anything you want. Somebody must like you."

"I don't think that's the case, Don. They just don't like you."

"Yeah, that's what I figured. Anyway, two boats were within sight nearby but only one was close enough to witness the incident. Their statements have been uploaded to the case file. You can read them on-line."

Tommy said, "Don, we'll read them but give us your version of what happened."

"The Eleanor is a sixty foot luxury yacht converted into a research ship. The team of marine biologists and a crew of three were scanning the ocean floor of the straight with some experimental 3D gizmo when the yacht was attacked."

Carlos asked, "What do you mean attacked?"

"Not exactly sure. The two boats close by heard excited radio traffic on the Coast Guard channel. The captain of the nearest boat saw the Eleanor rocking back and forth like it being shaken. Then he swears he saw an arm or tentacle or something reach over the side of the ship and start pulling it under."

"Excited how?" Tommy asked.

"Surprise maybe turning into panic. Here come the survivors. I'll let your team get their statements."

Steve, Carmen, and Carlos sat at separate booths to get the three survivors accounts of what happened.

"We got the scanning array working and we were all excited. The detail of the sea bed was totally amazing. Then we saw a movement on the floor and then the whole sea floor was in motion. It was coming up towards us and fast. Jarrod had been on the radio so he called the Coast Guard. We got hit and the boat jumped out of the water and landed on its side. None of us were wearing life-jackets. Skip and Randy got the jackets out and went below. We never saw them again."

"Who are Skip and Randy?"

"They worked on the boat."

"You said Jarrod was on the radio before he called the Coast Guard. Who was he talking to?"

"The Argus, the other boat we were working with and Kitsap Naval Base."

30 The Get Away

St. Rita's Catholic Church
Berriman Street, Brooklyn, New York
Saturday, October 8, 2011, 6:35 AM EDT

Andy's car pulled to the back of the church. Nina walked out of the auto recycling yard two doors down in dirty work clothes and a ball cap. The safety glasses looked ridiculous but got her to the car unnoticed.

"Father Rand said you could get me out of town."

"I can," Andy said. "I'll give you a choice. There is a good family outside Aspen Colorado who will take you in as long as you need or you can come with me to Seattle to hunt for the sea monster. Aspen is beautiful. The family is awesome. Seattle is rainy and I'll probably work with the FBI on this case they have going."

"I pick Seattle."

"Aspen is safe. Seattle is unknown and there are some difficult people involved."

"You're a billionaire. If I change my mind send me to Aspen."

31 Source Documents

Garty Publishing Offices
455 W 45th St, New York
Monday, October 8, 2011, 11:10 AM EDT

"Dis better not be some joke or I will trace this number and hurt you!"

"Is this Jimmy Swartko?"

"Who's asking?"

"Jimmy, this is agent Steven Haskins with the FBI. I'm calling about photos printed in all four of your tabloids, photos of the Seattle sea monster."

"Yeah well you gotta prove you're FBI cause I ain't buying it. You gotta come down here and show me a badge and I'll have a cop here to arrest you if you try impersonating anybody!"

"No problem, Jimmy. I'll have a team right over with a search warrant to comb through your pictures for anything inappropriate. It may take our team weeks and we will hold you personally liable for any pictures taken illegally or of illegal content. You will, of course, provide us with the details of every picture we question, details which you have at hand."

"Hey, no need to get personal. I gotta protect my sources from scams."

"You would know all about scams, Jimmy. I see in your record ..."

"Don't get huffy on me. I don't got the photos, not the original photos. You need to talk to a lawyer but he's in Seattle. He ain't here."

"What's his name, Jimmy, and phone number?"

32 Message

Dillon & Weygandt
315 Union St., Seattle, WA
Monday, October 10, 2011, 8:30 AM PDT

"Attorney Michael Weygandt, please."

"Attorney Weygandt is not available at the moment. Would you like to leave a message?"

"This is FBI agent Steven Haskins. I'm calling about . . ."

"The FBI! Attorney Weygandt has been waiting for your call. I can set up a meeting as soon as you are available."

"We can be in Seattle on Wednesday, early morning is best."

"I will schedule you for 8:00 AM."

33 Sail River

Sail River Inlet
State Route 112, Clallam County, WA
Saturday, October 8, 2011, 11:30 AM PDT

Carlos eyes went wide, "Andy? What are you doing here? You shouldn't be here. If Tommy sees you he is gonna blow a gasket."

"I told him the same thing," Steve said.

Carlos looked at the girl and back to Andy, "Is this the nun?"

"She's not a nun," Andy answered.

"I'm not a nun yet, I'm a novitiate," Nina corrected.

Andy said, "I thought you were going to quit?"

"I didn't quit yet," Nina snapped.

"Andy!"

Nina saw Andy tense as the woman approached. "Nina, this is Carmen."

Carmen coldly looked at Nina and back to Andy, "You leave now or I arrest you both for hindering a federal investigation."

"No, I was asked to see if I could help!"

Carmen pulled out handcuffs and said, "Did Steve put you up to this?"

Tommy walked into the open, "I asked Andy to stop by if he was available. Put your cuffs away."

Carlos cut in, "You said this investigation would be strictly by the book."

"Too many weird things going on here," Tommy said. "Andy's the best tour guide through the weird."

"Tour guide and main attraction," Steve said.

"But we just started, Tommy," Carmen countered. "We have enough people questioning our methods and sanity and we've covered this beach already. The police have covered it. Fifty three days after the event there is nothing left to see here!"

Tommy's eyebrows raised, "Who's questioning our sanity?"

Andy pointed to the man sitting on the beach wearing an old slicker, "Did anyone talk to that guy?"

The group turned to look at the empty beach. Carmen said, "Shit!"

"Here we go again," Carlos said.

Nina felt her sense of balance sliding in many directions. She instinctively grabbed for Andy's arm but missed as Andy started walking toward the beach. Carmen swatted Nina's hand away with an annoyed look. Carlos stepped up quickly offering his arm.

Andy sat next to the man who was staring at the horizon. He looked at the man and then also stared out to sea.

"What happened that night?" Andy asked.

The voice sounded hollow, far away, "I was looking for my father-in-law. I thought he was ... Something dark landed on me, held me down and crushed me, all of me. Tell my wife ... "

Andy cut him off, "You aren't fooling anyone. I know what you are."

Empty eye sockets turned toward Andy, "I fooled them because you saw me. You don't matter. If you want to know more solicit the lawyer."

What Tommy, Nina, and the team saw was Andy sit on a rock ledge say a few words and a man materialized next to him. Andy turned and said something. The man faded into mist blowing toward them with the on-shore breeze.

Steve quickly looked at Carmen. Given her history he wasn't sure if there was any lingering effects. Carmen's eye were wide. Steve assumed panic. Nina froze except for the involuntary muscle spasms shaking her face and arms. Soon her knees buckled and she went down. Carlos' eyes darted about. Steve caught Carmen wiping tears.

34 Forms of Torture

Cambourne Hall, Library Room
  Near Oxford, England
  Tuesday, October 11, 2011, 4:20 PM GMT

Alicia's mother, Congresswoman Macy Montgomery, was amazingly helpful when she wanted something. This was not one of those times.

"You're on your own there, Pumpkin. I'm herding panicky politicians toward a hot branding iron. Best of luck, though," Macy yelled into the speaker phone from across a room full of staffers.

Alicia completed the last on-line form. The paper forms completed faxing to New York and Washington DC. The FBI, SEC, and a dozen other federal agencies had been officially notified. Alicia had to go through this process but the discussions, the options selected, the investigative steps all felt weightless, like the slightest whim of a bureaucrat, a bad lunch, lost relationship, burnt toast, anything could derail each and every process. She needed something solid.

"Moira," Alicia called. "Moira, do you remember the picture the FBI sent for a wedding present?"

"Yes, Mum."

"There is a business card tucked into the frame. Will you bring it to me?"

"Yes, Mum."

Moira returned with the card. Alicia turned the card around remembering taking the card from Alan's desk in New York. The same day she threatened to dent Sir Smythley's head with the paper weight. Angela laughed and cheered. The memory made Alicia smile. That was the end of July, only three months ago. Angela was so alive. So much had happened since. Alicia looked down at her hands now remembering Angela's blood covering them. She wiped the tears and dialed the number.

35 Huddle Time

Smugglers Landing Restaurant
Port Angeles, Washington
Tuesday, October 11, 2011, 1:55 PM PDT

Tommy pulled out his cell surprised to see Alicia's name on the incoming call. He let it roll to voice mail saying, "Team, this is Mark Ohashi. He is our new forensics specialist."

Welcomes all around and then Tommy continued, "Steve, what did you find out?"

"Eight AM tomorrow at the lawyer's office, downtown Seattle. Apparently, he is excited to talk to us."

Tommy said, "Excited lawyers are looking for a payday. Carlos, you and I will take the meeting."

The team sat by the windows facing the harbor. Nina sat two tables away listening and watching Carmen.

"Okay Andy, out with it. What happened on the beach? What was that thing?"

Andy said, "I know you don't like the word demon but ..."

Steve cut in, "If a dead ten foot Celtic priestess fits the bill, I'm good with what ever you want to call it."

Andy continued, "I'm guessing it was trying to look like the man who died. Anyway, it didn't mind that I knew what it was. It only said something dark landed on him and held him down, then crushed him."

Tommy said, "Mark, what was the cause of death?"

"Blunt force trauma is an understatement. Almost every bone was fractured, even fingers and toes. Loose stones on the beach should have protected some bones. I saw a body run over by a steam roller with less damage. The site was well trampled, no foot prints found not even giant foot prints."

Tommy glared, but Mark said, "Hey, we know people are going to ask, besides a giant would never get under the high tension wires between the beach and the road."

"What position was the body in?" Steve asked.

"Looks like he was standing facing whatever crushed him and fell straight back. He didn't even turn his head."

"Carmen, for the yacht attack, go over the interview recordings and make call backs. Scour every fact to re-create the scene. Steve and Mark, go over to the boat repair and look over the yacht. It's in a warehouse over there," Tommy said pointing out the window past the ferry landing.

Andy said, "There was another thing, Tommy. That thing on the beach said something about us getting evidence from the lawyer."

"Something? What exactly did it say?"

"We should ask the the lawyer."

Carmen said, "No, it said solicit the lawyer."

All eyes turned to Carmen. Tommy said, "So you heard that thing."

She added, "I don't know any more. He was blowing away and it kind of shook me.

Carlos said, "We will talk to the lawyer tomorrow. It only shook you a little? I can't believe I didn't crap my pants."

Steve said, "Carlos, we're all surprised you didn't crap your pants. Ohashi huh? You don't look Irish."

Carmen said, "You can ignore him. We do."

36 Alicia

Smugglers Landing Restaurant
  Port Angeles, Washington
  Tuesday, October 11, 2011, 2:35 PM PDT

"Alicia, I saw your call. Great to hear from you!"

"Tommy, thank you so much for the picture and t-shirt. It made me cry and miss you all."

"How's married life?"

"Alan is amazing and the home is a castle but it's hard for a potato farmer's daughter to be proper all the time. I had no idea it would be so hard. I do have some good people reminding me all – the – time."

"Alicia, I'm glad you called and I'm hoping it's just to catch up, but I don't think so."

"No Tommy, I need some advise and maybe a recommendation. Random's father may have stolen from Celestina's family. Stocks were purchased and sold but the funds never came back to the Cassanzo's accounts."

"Cassanzos are asking you to pay the money back?"

"They want the money back, but the money is still draining. A representative from the family named Salvatore threatened Alan in order to make it stop. People in the village here said this Salvatore tortured someone at the house already. I'm sure it's just gossip but this man has the look of a killer."

"I wish I had better news, Alicia, but the man is a killer. He can be a nice guy when he needs to be. Don't be fooled. He did torture someone and left him at your house. I am assuming you are trying all the official channels and are now looking for alternative help. You should call your mother."

"I tried. Her hands are full already."

"I know a few people that might be able to help. Let me ask around."

"I would really appreciate it, Tommy"

"I'll call back tomorrow to tell you what I find."

"Thank you, Tommy. Tell everyone I said hello."

37 Thug

New York, NY
    Tuesday, October 11, 2011, 6:15 PM EDT

"Hey Alan, 'ow you doin'? Not every day I get a call from a British Lord. What can I do for you?"

-

Roscoe Tanner listened intently sitting in the back booth of Mazarella's Corner Bar. His usual office when not at home.

-

"So you got someone else's money and problems dat go with it. First thing you gotta know is that you gotta make this right. This ain't one guy leaning on ya. It's a whole organization. Second thing is keep your priorities straight. The goal is to live through dis. If you gotta pay then you pay, keep your lady safe. Third thing, money transfers leave trails all over the place. In time someone can track 'em down. The trick here is to find the right guy to do the tracking."

-

"Uh huh, how about your British buddies? You know guys over there with money."

-

"Oh, and that's why you're calling me. You money types play rough. I know guys who can find the money but not people you want to do

business with. They help you – they own you, like dat. Lemme check
with one of my professors, see if I can give you another option."

-

"Hey, one more thing, since we talked in that bar in Jersey City, the day
we met Jimmy?"

-

"Yeah, that day. I started working on my masters thesis again cause of
you. Thank you for dat."

-

"Doan mention it. Talk to you soon, Alan."

38 Dry Dock

Washington Marine Repair
Port Angeles, Washington
Tuesday, October 11, 2011, 2:35 PM PDT

"I can do that for you."

Steve snarled, "Keep your eyes on the road."

Mark said, "I have face recognition software. Take about ten minutes."

"I don't have a face, only a hunch."

As Mark pulled into Marine Repair's lot he said, "You're comparing two videos. I can compare the videos and give you a percent match for each person in the videos using head shape, hair texture, hair line, shoulders, whatever shows. It can narrow the number of people you need to compare. What are you comparing?"

"A murder scene and an airport terminal."

The two men walked into to large metal building next to the bay. A scent mixture of sea spray and dirty oil met them. A gravely voice barked at them, "Hey, read the sign! No customers in the shop. You'll have to wait outside."

Steve flipped open his badge, "FBI, I'm here to see the boat from Neah Bay."

"Sure, hang on a sec. It's outside."

In a row of vessels the mechanic started to pull canvas off the bow and side of a long sleek white hull. Mark said, "Where's the damage?"

Steve said, "Hey, can we get this moved into the warehouse and out of the rain?"

39 Observations

Smugglers Landing Restaurant
   Port Angeles, Washington
   Tuesday, October 11, 2011, 2:45 PM PDT

"She's lying."

Andy said, "No, she was right. That thing used the word solicit."

"Not what I meant. Carmen doesn't look at you and when she does her eyes go wide, and you know what that means. She saw that thing on the beach and was ignoring it until you said something and no one called her on it. It's like everyone's afraid of her. They are strong people. It doesn't make sense. She acts all tough but she's afraid. That's what she's lying about."

"This team had their beliefs, jobs, everything about their lives turned inside out constantly in the last four months. We lost Angela in Foley Square. Carmen was possessed by demons she didn't believe in. Carlos had his most intimate thoughts violated. Tommy got his soul shredded and barely escaped, Steve disappeared into some dimension and came back with a vicious tattoo. They are all still in shock. Yes, they're all hiding. I think they don't confront Carmen because they don't want to lose her. She, them, they're all still fragile. What ever she is hiding she will need admit it. First step to recovery, right?"

Nina said, "Hmm, I never thought of that.

"Besides, you're the only one who fainted."

Nina said, "Yeah, but I recovered. They didn't go down but they still haven't recovered. It seems like Steve is the only one who's handled it well."

Andy said, "Steve got his tattoo instead of having a pen go through his head but, you're right about Steve. He seems almost human these days."

40 Dry Dock – part 2

Washington Marine Repair
Port Angeles, Washington
Tuesday, October 11, 2011, 3:50 PM PDT

"There it is," Mark said angling the light stand up into the gap in the hull. "Now I can start. Steve, finish setting up the taller light towers and I'll start collecting samples."

The mechanic told Steve, "We're leaving in five minutes. Make sure you turn off the lights and lock the door you came in. The rig holding the boat is strong but no jumping or dancing up there."

Steve said, "Quick question before you leave, with a opening in the hull like that how come this didn't go straight to the bottom?"

The mechanic reached into the gash in the hull and lifted up a canvas inside the cabin, "This is a float bag. There is a whole system of 'em around the interior cabins. One of the crew had the presence of mind to trip the CO_2 cartridges to inflate the bags. Even if a couple of the bags were punctured this boat wouldn't sink for days."

"How would you make a hole like this if you were trying?"

"Me? This is a closed cell composite made with primary bonded resins and skinned with aluminum. Very tough, light, and flexible. The only way I know to make a hole in it is to drill. I could shoot a hole with a fifty caliber machine gun and full ammo box. To bash a hole? I have no idea without explosives. Tough question."

Mark said, "The opening is forty inches long and nine inches at the widest. Like a long oval and flaring inward like a stab not like a cut or drilled opening, and what do we have here? Steve, hand me the evidence bags."

The mechanic said, "I can see you're in for a long night. I got to take off. My son's playing Bremerton tonight and it's a long drive. We'll see you tomorrow."

41 Behind the Scenes

FBI Headquarters
935 Pennsylvania Avenue, NW
Washington, D.C.
Tuesday, October 11, 2011, 7:10 PM EDT

Deputy Director Tristano said, "Nate, their budget was approved by the Director and the White House. Be patient. People will forget. They'll move on to the next news story."

CIRG section chief, Nathaniel Rorbach said, "I know a short cut. One of the team has a facial tattoo. It looks disgusting. Kick him out on appearance violations and the team will crumble."

"Tommy would request another agent."

"Agents wouldn't want to work for Tommy. His task force is getting the x file reputation. Serious agents will keep away."

Tristano pointed to a thick folder on a side board, "That folder gets thicker every day with requests to join Serial Events Task Force."

Rorbach answered, "I talk to agents every day complaining about them ruining our reputation."

42 Temporary Office Space

123 West 1st Street
  Port Angeles, WA
  Tuesday, October 11, 2011, 9:15 PM PDT

"The agents around here think you're ruining the FBI's name," Mark said, "but all the tech support staff are fighting to work with you!"

"That explains the weird looks," Steve said.

Carlos said, "And the crap assignments."

Carmen said, "Steve, all you get is weird looks."

"Back on track, people!" Tommy said. "So the research boat looks like an animal or something struck it. Keep in mind that our job is to solve one death first, Mr. Tony McCarty. Next we go after the four deaths on the research boat. We are not, I repeat, not ghost hunting, sea monster hunting, big foot or vampire hunting. If credible evidence leads to investigating in a particular area we follow the leads. Also, I told, I mean asked, Andy and the nun to keep away from us and the press."

Steve said, "So they're confined to their hotel room? Very cozy."

Tommy ignored him and said, "Carmen, what did the U.S. Navy say?"

Carmen glared at Steve and said, "I left messages with the public spokesperson's office and with the Naval Undersea Warfare Center. No response yet."

Steve said, "We are tipping around in their backyard. Trust me, they are very aware of what is going on. When we get too close they will find us."

Steve said, "Oh, one insignificant detail, Tommy. Ohashi compared some video for me. A kid followed me from the crime scene in San Fran

83

to the airport. I'm pretty sure he followed me here. I think it's the LBH from Zuccotti Park."

"LBH?" Carlos said.

"Light blue hoodie," Carmen answered.

43 Morning Alarm

Cambourne Hall, Master Bed Room
  Near Oxford, England
  Wednesday, October 12, 2011, 6::00 AM GMT

Alicia woke to the sound of falling glass and her alarm. She switched it off as the second bullet pierced the window and embedded high over Alicia's head, a few inches below the first shot. Alicia dove for the floor scrambling around to the far side of the bed. She popped up and grabbed her husband's arm and rolled him off the bed on top of her, his feet still tangled in sheets. The third bullet crashed through the window frame before cratering the wall.

Sixty seconds later from inside the Butler's pantry a frantic call was made to Italy, "Salvatore, what the hell are you doing!"

"Lord St. Claire, Alan, good to hear from you. I am relaxing on my veranda in the morning sun."

Alan said, "You bastard! You shot into our bedroom! We are doing all we can do! This is taking time!"

"It was probably just a wake up call but, you have given me nothing to tell my employer. My employer is running out of time. Our money is still disappearing. You will find it quickly or the bullets will be lower next time, and your house has many windows."

44 The Cardshark Speaks

Washington D.C.
    The Watergate Hotel
    Wednesday, October 12, 2011, 1:10 AM EDT

Macy Montgomery said, "Honey, I hear you just fine. Calm yourself. Your daddy is here and you know how grumpy he gets when his sleep is interrupted."

-

"Hold on, let me get to my laptop."

-

Macy Montgomery plugged her headphone in and started typing.
    "Alice honey, I'm checking now. The gal at SEC says your requests haven't been touched. Here's another email from Justice. Looks like the same at Justice."

-

"The sniffing around I did yesterday showed me no one wants to talk about your problem. If you ask me, this smells like Mr. Harriman figured out you're not on his side."

***

In the windowless Butlers Pantry in England Alicia sat on the stone floor with Alan listening to the master politician's advice.

Alicia hung up the phone and said, "Mom told me all the decks are stacked against us. No help is coming from SEC, the banks, or the courts."

"Then what does she suggest?" Alan said.

"She told me we need to reshuffle the deck. Befriend enemies, cut ties to questionable friends, call in favors, and shake the bushes to see what falls out. She also said a little crazy goes a long way."

Alan nodded, "Right then. Call MacKenna. Get our house and property under control. I'm going to shake the Lord Chancellor to get traction on this investigation."

"Oooo, I love it when you get bossy."

"Not now, love. The game's afoot."

45 The Eavesdrop

The Game Room
   London, England
   Wednesday, October 12, 2011, 6:12 AM GMT

"He doesn't know Clark is out. Make certain Hopkins does not get through to him. That will slow him down enough. Wait two days then follow through. The only real advantage he had left was his wife's connections."

"I'd heard you retired. So glad you're back on the job."

"I wouldn't miss it. This one is personal," Sir Wynton Smyley said.

46 MacKenna

"Gregor will leave, no question. Grady will stay, she's been through it before in Ireland. If Grady stays Moira stays. The rest o" the staff, I canno' guess. We'll need to get on a war footing, fix the windows and walls upstairs, get a proper cleaner in here. I know a lad in East Midlands I can bring in for a few days. It would be prudent to inventory the gun room and its lot. Can your ladyship handle a gun?"

"Shotguns and rifles, yes. My father took me hunting every fall."

"But did ya' ever hit anything?"

"I wouldn't shoot a deer, but I got two pheasants my first time out, and I shot a rabid dog once."

"Oh wale, that's something! And no more jogging around the park for you. We'll get you a treadmill for the dungeon. You'll need better lighting, and some exercise equipment. We'll also need to upgrade electric service and internet, trim down the bushes in the front, reinforce the ..."

47 Hiding Clark

Red Lion Pub
  London, England
  Wednesday, October 12, 2011, 11:30 AM GMT

"What you want 'im for then?"

Alan said through gritted teeth, "Look, I've been all over Parliment. I know he is in London. He's been seen. I just need to talk to him. Do you know where the Chancellor is?"

"Oh, Ken Clark's not Chancellor no more, didn't cha hear?"

"What? When did this happen?"

"Read your newspapers, mate. Some ridiculous row about expenses. Yeah, ain't turned in 'is robes yet but he's bagged."

"Who is the new Chancellor then?"

"Tories are still in power so Sir Brian Crighton, of course."

"Of Blackford Crighton, certainly."

"Hey, don't look so down. He's a descent chap. What's your beef?"

Alan shook his head, "He's my old boss."

"Well, you got an in with him then. Good for you."

"No, he sacked me."

48 Small Steps and Favors

"James Hayden, Ma'am."

"James, glad to meet you. You came very quickly. How soon can you start?"

MacKenna said, "James completed the first pass a short time ago. He wanted to start right away because you promised him an extra hundred quid. Quid means pounds."

"I promised him that? That was very smart of me."

"Yes Ma'am. Your ladyship is very clever about these things," MacKenna said.

"What did you find? Can we discuss it here?"

James said, "Yes Ma'am. This room, well the whole ground floor is clean except for the Butler's Pantry which had two bugs. Aindroo told me you wanted to leave one of 'em just in case."

Alicia looked slyly at Aindroo and said, "There I go being clever again."

"That you are, your ladyship," MacKenna said. "The only problem is we will have to convince the party on the other end that we are no' onto that one."

James said, "I still need to sweep the upper floors and we need to discuss where you want a control room."

Just then the housekeeper's door opened and Alan entered head down.

"Oh dear, what now?" Alicia said.

"Clark is out. We've lost our sponsorship on the council. It appears the doors are closing all over London."

Alicia thought then said, "Alan, step into the butler's pantry. I want to discuss our wedding reception."

Alan shook his head, "Don't think I can manage it, dear."

Alicia took Alan's hand and said, "I can help you. I've been saving a special treat."

Aindroo put a large paw on James shoulder guiding him away from the kitchen and pantry. Mrs. Grady called out from the servants hall, "Should have put a couch in there, MacKenna."

"Don't need a couch," MacKenna said, "since her ladyship replaced the old chair with a padded one and no arms. Why, Mrs. Grady, you suddenly look flushed!"

"What are you on about? Get on with your business, old man!"

49 The Lawyer

Dillon & Weygandt Offices
315 Union St., Seattle, WA
Wednesday, October 12, 2011, 8:00 AM PDT

"Gentlemen, I'm Michael Weygandt. Thank you for seeing me. Can I see your warrant for the photos?"

Tommy said, "We don't have one but if that is a problem I can get one delivered in fifteen minutes."

"Maybe, but first I would like to make a proposal. You are looking for evidence. The photos may or may not be evidence for the Tony McCarty murder."

"It is not a murder yet," Carlos said.

"Still, you are looking for evidence. I have the original photos but I have even better evidence. Let me state for the record, I will cooperate with the FBI to the fullest extent."

Tommy said, "We need to talk to John Watson, the captain."

"That's me! I am the captain of the sail boat John Watson. The photos I gave to the press are worth a fortune. They are provocative but not conclusive. I would like to keep them. In exchange I have better evidence. I have transcripts of eyewitness accounts from myself, my wife and my son. I have the ship's log and transcripts of radio communications before, during, and after the event. I have GPS readings, the correct ones, not what the media made up. Best of all, I have video recording of the incident you will probably want to suppress. What do you say?"

Tommy said, "We will have to review the evidence first. Even then I cannot promise we won't need the original photos."

"I have the video cued up in the conference room. No one, other than my wife, son, and myself have seen it. Let's watch."

50 Autograph Hound

Gastroburger
    Port Angeles, WA
    Wednesday, October 12, 2011, 11:35 AM PDT

"Hey Cutie!" Steve said.

"Hey tall, blue, and handsome."

You know Sandy, I could see more of you if I stayed at your place."

"Well Steve, the answer is the same as the last six times you asked. If you want me, you need to take all of me," Sandy leaned in close blowing into his ear, "and I will drive you absolutely wild." Steve's eyes fluttered and misted over.

Sandy followed with, "By the way lover, you have a fan over there that wants you to autograph her beer bottle, the skinny little girl in the huskies jersey."

Steve approached the table. The girl with black hair and glasses said, "I love the face. Can't forget a face like that."

"Thanks, I can sign your bottle but I'm seeing someone."

The girl pulled an empty Blue Face IPA bottle and a felt pen from a pocket and said, "You aren't my type."

Steve signed while the girl said wistfully, "Larry Mastkowski was my type."

51 Hydrophones

123 West 1st Street
  Port Angeles, WA
  Wednesday, October 12, 2011, 12:40 PM PDT

"Good afternoon team. This is Doctor Abigail Palmero, University oceanography department. Abby was the advisor to the seafloor scanning project."

"Not past tense, Tommy. I still am the team's advisor. The three survivors don't want to quit, but we need to follow scientific method. We have the partial sea bed scan the yacht Eleanor made."

Mark Ohashi said, "The hard drives on the Eleanor were trashed. We'll need a clean room to read them."

Abby said, "The Argus has a copy of all but the last twenty seconds. The ships were working together. I asked the project leader to compile the scans and get the strait's hydrophone recordings."

"Hydrophone, you mean underwater microphones. Do they pick up shipping traffic?"

"It's possible. It would be background noise. You need a lot of filtering to get to it plus a baseline to compare against, and that assumes the Hydrophones are turned on."

"Turned on?" Tommy asked.

"Sure, the military turns them off randomly to disguise their traffic in and out of Puget Sound. They control them remotely from the Kitsap base. The ridiculous thing is, the recording equipment is stored in a shed on a public pier in Port Townsend, secured with a paddle lock and chain. Anyone can get to the equipment." Abby added, "If the recordings are available they're on line. We can download them any time. What are you looking for?"

"August seventeenth, around midnight. Tony McCarty was crushed on a beach around that time."

52 Guidance

Office Space, 123 West 1st Street
  Port Angeles, WA
  Wednesday, October 12, 2011, 1:05 PM PDT

Tommy said, "Okay, the doctor is gone. Carlos, text Andy to get over here. Steve, what did you find?"

Steve pulled out an old clock radio and switched it on. Loud static filled the office as Steve motioned everyone to gather around the eight foot conference table. As they sat down a young girl came out of the back rooms and sat in a middle seat next to Steve.

Tommy said, "Who is this?"

"LBH, light blue hoodie."

"You can call me Holly."

"What can we do for you, Holly?" Tommy said.

"I'm here to trade information for protection."

"We are no longer investigating Invade Wall Street, but we can put you in touch with ... "

"No, I work with Steve or I walk."

Carmen put handcuffs on the table and said, "We can arrest you now and turn you over to White Collar Crimes Unit."

Steve said, "Whoa, slow down Carmen, Tommy. So far all we know is that she took part in a peaceful protest. White Collar can't match her photo or prints to any database. She is off the grid."

"If you arrest me I get held for twenty four hours max, then released, and I'm gone. You get nothing."

Tommy said, "What information are we buying? I make no deals without verification. Even if the information is good what's the cost?"

"I need out of the country, no paper work."

"What you are asking is illegal."

Holly shrugged, "An empty seat on a military transport, Navy ship, government flight over seas, they leave the US all the time. I give you the big picture with a couple details for verification; you ship me out; then I fill in the rest of the details. Believe me, you will want to make this deal."

53 Verification

The Game Room
  London, England
  Wednesday, October 12, 2011, 9:15 PM GMT

The phone connected but no one responded. The operator gave his report without delay, per instructions.

"Sir, we have verification. All audio units are unresponsive with one exception. All video units are unresponsive, no exceptions."

"The working unit is in the kitchen and in the butler's pantry. The pantry is the communications hub for the house. We believe it is still undiscovered because of near by comm and electrical wires, also, intimate conversations were recorded at 2:55 PM."

-

"Yes Sir, very intimate."

54 LBH Offer

Office Space
   Port Angeles, WA
   Wednesday, October 12, 2011, 1:30 PM PDT

"Tommy, before we shut her down let's hear the big picture. If we are interested Holly can give us details to verify."

Andy knocked and was let in with Nina. "Sorry Andy, she can't be here. I'm taking a big risk with you."

"I can't leave her, Tommy. I promised to keep her safe."

Steve said, "She can wait in the back office. There's no doors or windows."

"Sounds charming," Nina said.

Andy said, "You can still choose Aspen."

"I'm going, I'm going."

Tommy said to Nina, "After Holly is done she will join you. Andy, this is Holly. She has information on another case. Okay Holly, you're on. Tell us the big picture."

"This is about power, political and economic. I only know about the money part. We recruit banks and stock trading companies to participate, then we loot their transactions. I've been working on it for two years. The people are well armed and well funded. I put money into accounts for corporations, governments, and some individuals. Some are well known, some unknown. I can tell you there's a major play going on in Seattle. You're very close if you want do something about it."

Tommy said, "Okay, global conspiracies are nice, but let's bring this down earth a bit. We don't investigate conspiracies outside US borders. Give me something I can work with. You said you recruit banks. How does that work?"

"Too far into the details. I can tell you Larry was killed because he was trying to rescue me. Big players are in Seattle trying to close a backdoor I created. Before they figure out how to close the back door I can give you current transaction data and some history. After the door is closed I'll only have history. When I'm dead you get nothing."

Carlos said, "Why Seattle? They could close your backdoor from anywhere."

Holly's said, "You'd think so, wouldn't you?"

"Larry's death, that's one verifiable fact. Give me another one," Tommy said.

Okay, here's one you'll appreciate. I saw you on TV talking about her. I stole Celestina Cassanzo's money."

Holly then said, "Hmm, based on your sudden silence I guess we have a deal."

55 Colossus Revisited

Port Angeles, WA
Wednesday, October 12, 2011, 2:35 PM PDT

Holly joined Nina in the back room and Steve said, "Anything you show me now will seem anticlimactic next to that revelation.

Carlos set up his laptop and all gathered around. Tommy said, "you saw the photos in the papers. This is the video the captain's wife took. Before you watch this remember that we are looking for evidence for the cause of death of Tony McCarty. The GPS coordinates from the captain's log, verified by two shore stations, place the boat close to the middle of the straight, past Neah Bay and not quite to Sail River. Also, the first time through the sound is turned off. Second time Carlos will add the sound. Carlos, play it."

The screen went dark. The camera pointed down at gum boots then up to the window. A hand reached forward from the camera operator knocking on the window.

The hand began frantically pointing ahead into darkness past the ship's lit deck. Lightning bolts ripped through the clouds. In the middle of the screen a large shadow blocked the glow. The camera was shaking making focus difficult. The back of captain's rain slicker could be seen. A hand grabbed the camera and the image steadied. Lightning flashed again but this time it struck the object causing fire to run in red lava streaks across its surface. Without slowing its progress the face turned back to the direction of the lighting. A face, neither human nor animal, crossed by lines of flame looked back then down at the boat then forward again. The next flash of lighting showed nothing but wind and rain.

"Okay, I was wrong." Steve said. "That was wild."

"Any comments, Andy?"

"Let's watch it with sound first"

"Carlos, go ahead"

As soon as the gum boots were seen two people were yelling at each other.

Tommy said, "The voices you hear are the captain's wife and son."

Tommy's team heard a background of raging wind then the frantic conversation.

Son: It's there, right there! Look at the waves breaking!

Wife: Where, where?

Son: Dad, look out, turn around.

Wife: (knocking on the window) Mike, Mike, behind you! Look up there!

Thunder drowned out some words.

Son: Mom, point the camera higher! Kneel down if you have to.

Both: multiple exclamations

Lightning struck the creature followed by a noise similar to a roar but deeper, louder, deafening.

56 Analysis

Andy shook his head complaining, "If you want me to be sure of what you're showing me, and be absolutely certain, give me things I know about. I've seen demons as big as houses but this is a skyscaper, a mountain! The only thing I've heard of this big is an angel at the end of the world straddling sea and land."

"Tommy, this isn't getting us anywhere," Steve said. "We need to give him all the pieces."

"Okay, fill him in."

***

"I know you," Holly said. "I wasn't sure until I saw the look you gave the billionaire. You're that nun."

"You're not wrong, but probably not a nun, not ever."

"And you're sad about that? I couldn't stand feeling locked up. Can't go where you want, always praying, dressing the same way every day. You're like God's military."

Nina said, "Oh yeah? What's your story? You're not selling girl scout cookies, with your black hair and long face, hanging out with these guys. I got a home. I got family worried about me. They're spitting mad right now but there's a place at the dinner table. I work with the homeless every day. I can spot 'em and you are one of 'em. You dress nicer but you got the look."

Holly stopped her pacing. She turned away and sat facing a wall.

"Hey look," Nina said, "yeah, I'm sorry. I come out swinging cause I'm from Brooklyn. It's in the water or something, but I'm not wrong and I can tell it eats at you every day, I know. You act all tough. You been doing this a long time, and you're used to the life. There are ways out. Maybe I can help."

Holly wiped tears and said, "You can't help me. I have all the money I want and I'll be dead in a week or a year. No one will miss me or even know my real name."

"Hey, look at me," Nina said. "I promise, I'll remember you, and I'll pray for you. I'm a nun, what else can I do?"

Holly started sobbing. Nina put an arm around her shoulders.

57 Possibilities

Office Space
  Port Angeles, WA
  Wednesday, October 12, 2011, 3:05 PM, PDT

"I thought angels were fat little cupids with wings," Carlos said, "or they looked like regular people."

Andy said, "The angels I've seen were like people. They didn't scare me, but they scared everyone else. They were calm except for Warren. He was obnoxious." Andy glanced at Carmen who had her eyes closed.

"Did you ever see Warren again?" Steve asked.

"No, not after Celeste's funeral. We talk about angels like they are a single species. There are different kinds. Seraphs are one kind. Their name means 'burning ones.' I always thought they would be scary to meet. Some have multiple faces and arms. Some are full of eyes."

Tommy broke in, "Okay, you got us to believe in spirits or whatever. Give us some direction or context, otherwise we're wasting time. How can this relate to this case?"

Andy said, "The giant thing could either be some kind of angel or demon. It was headed toward Sail River. It let the boat see it. What did that accomplish? The thing on the beach, I'm pretty sure it was a demon. It felt evil. It was insulting. If it was a demon then its purpose is to deceive. Even truth it tells us is to deceive. I think just being on the beach was the goal. Which doesn't make any sense. I was the only one who saw it, right? Carmen, you only heard it until it melted away."

Carlos said, "The boat saw the giant and posted the photos. The photos brought the big crowd in. The crowd guaranteed the local forces couldn't handle the situation and the FBI would get the call."

"Why the FBI? What does that accomplish?" Tommy asked. "I'm not buying this connection."

58 Food to Go

Office
Port Angeles, WA
Wednesday, October 12, 2011, 3:05 PM, PDT

Steve took the bag of burgers and tray of drinks from the counter and a last kiss from Sandy.

"See you soon, soldier."

"Not soon enough," Steve said and then left.

A few minutes later a man walked up with his check, a hundred dollar bill, and a Russian accent, "You very pretty. The tattoo man, he likes you. He is lucky man. Keep change."

"Now, that is not necessary, but I thank you," Sandy smiled sweetly putting the money into the cash drawer. The man and three others with him walked out, Brandon, the other bar tender, walked out behind them and passed the SUV they climbed into without looking their way and headed to the grocery. Brandon returned from the grocery store and placed a bag on the bar and said, "Here you go, Sandy," handing her the receipt. She flipped it over. Brandon wrote the make, model, and plate number on the back.

Sandy pulled out her cell, "Steve, you had another admirer today."

-

"No, a guy, a guy with a Russian accent, military haircut, paid in cash."

-

"Yes, six foot even, maybe two hundred. He also had long sleeves but I caught a tattoo where the thumb and index finger join, three small circles touching each other."

-

"No, he was nice, left a huge tip."

-

"You're welcome, honey. You can also thank my Ex if you ever meet."

59 Holly

Office Space
Port Angeles, WA
Wednesday, October 12, 2011, 5:00 PM, PDT

"Tommy, we have a problem," Steve said. "Sandy just told me some guys with Russian accents spotted me. We need to talk to Holly now!"

Tommy opened the door to the back office. Holly and Nina were eating burgers and chatting. "Holly, why are there Russians outside looking for us?"

"No! No, they can't be! They're in Seattle!"

Steve said, "They were eating two doors down at the gastroburger just a few minutes ago, and they were asking about me."

Holly started looking around frantically.

"Holly, I am assuming that if any of us walk out the front door or climb out a window we'll be dead in seconds. Am I correct? Am I correct!"

Holly sobbed. Steve knelt and grabbed her arms. "Holly, what will they do? What weapons do they have?"

Holly looked to Nina, but Steve demanded, "Holly, or what ever your name is, I am not dying here! What did you do?"

Tommy ordered, "Carlos, call Port Angeles Police. Give them the details. Tell them to approach cautiously."

Nina cried out, "She was their prisoner! She was kidnapped! This is not her fault! Leave her alone!"

Tommy knelt next to Steve, "Holly, we are out of time. What is going on?"

"They hired me to hack a bank. They said they would pay me, but then they made me hack a payment processor. They wouldn't let me go. They threatened to kill me if I tried to escape or told anyone. We were in New York, in the park. When Steve made everyone run away I escaped from them and hid."

"So you know what they did, and they want to hurt you. Why are they after Steve?"

"I don't know. Maybe they are following him to find me."

Tommy said, "That's not enough. What do they want? What else is going on?"

"I stole their money. After I got away in New York I used secret tunnels to hide their money. I wanted to make sure they would leave me alone. Larry was trying to help me. He was going to meet them to give them their money back, but they pulled up to his car in the parking lot and shot him in the head!" Holly's sobbing renewed, "They didn't even talk to him!"

"Holly, how much money did you take from them?"

"I don't know. I never added it up. It's all in different accounts and it moves all the time."

"Are we talking millions?"

"There are millions in each account, sometimes hundreds of millions."

Carlos said, "Cruisers are on the way. Holly, what do you mean by secret tunnels?"

"It's dark net connections. They're not listed anywhere. You just have to know about them."

"Why is the backdoor in Seattle?" Steve said.

"Because I hard coded it into some network appliance they were installing in Seattle. Seattle has an IXP with direct connections to China and Japan."

Tommy said, "What is an IXP and how do we find it?"

60 Response

6:00 AM the alarm sounded in the master bedroom. The lady in the master bedroom rose from the bed. Glass shards popped out from a window pane. The wall darkened with red spatters behind the lady as she fell.

The sniper descended from the tree stand, placed the barrel, scope, and stock into their separate spaces in the case. He climbed into a van, pulled onto the road and left.

61 Chaos and Orders

Cambourne
Thursday, October 13, 2011, 6:15 AM GMT

"Where is she? Mrs. Hodson, her royal highness has not come down yet. Will you shake the feathers out of her head?" Mrs. Grady asked.

Ten minutes later a scream was heard that woke Alan and Alicia sleeping in a windowless room.

Alicia fell against Alan sobbing, "It's my fault, I didn't shut off the alarm when we moved bedrooms." Moira's body fell with her reaching for the still ringing alarm.

Mrs. Grady rushed into the room, paused, and flung herself on Moira wailing inconsolably.

Alan noticed the broken glass on the floor and walked Alicia out of the room. "Gregor, call the police. Alicia, I need you to get hold of MacKenna. I'm calling Salvatore"

Gregor said, "Sir, after the police leave I will be leaving your employ. Under the circumstances, you will forgive me if I don't wait for a replacement to be found."

Alicia said through her tears, "Of course Gregor, we understand, but we will expect you at the funeral."

Gregor nodded, "Yes Ma'am."

62 Discovery

The Game Room, London
Thursday, October 13, 2011, 6:15 AM GMT

"Confirmed, Sir Smythley, the target is still moving."

-

"Yes sir, not for long."

63 Calling Salvatore

Near Rome

Thursday, October 13, 2011, 6:20 AM GMT +1

"Signore please ... Signore, Alan, I have no reason to harm your wife"

-

"I needed you to understand ..."

-

"Tell me what happened."

-

"I assure you no one in my organization or my employer's had any hand in this ..."

-

"Lord St. Claire, the safety of your home, I will make it my priority. I will reach out to resources today."

64 After Thought

Port Angeles Police Station
Port Angeles, WA
Wednesday, October 12, 2011, 10:25 PM PDT

The team sat in a small meeting room in the police station. Tommy, Steve, and company sat at a large table. Nina and Holly talked quietly at the far end of the room with Holly crying occasionally.

Tommy announced he would be driving Holly back to Seattle. Andy said, "The two things seem related is all I'm saying. The big thing was moving toward Sail River based on the sighting and probable direction and a crushed body on the beach."

Steve said, "So Priss, what you're saying is a giant walks through the strait, comes on shore and stomps Tony McCarty, whose only crime is having a father-in-law with dementia. Then where does the giant go?"

Tommy's cell vibrated again.

Carmen said, "The creature is not walking at least not on the bottom. Assuming basic dimensions of a human or animal, it's feet would go two, maybe three hundred feet down. The depth is about six fifty."

"She does speak!" Steve said to Carmen. "I was wondering when you'd come back to us."

Mark Ohashi said, "The giant couldn't go inland from there. There's high tension lines close to the beach. You can see them on the satellite view. Look."

"Playing limbo with the power lines probably wouldn't work," Carlos said.

All looked at the laptop. Steve said, "Oh shit! I was standing right there and didn't see it." Steve pointed at the high tension lines, "Right there! It's an access road from the beach to the highway. I don't know if that thing came ashore, but it's ideal for a landing craft."

"To land what?" Tommy said while glancing again at his cell phone.

"Good question, but try this scenario; a landing craft comes ashore, hits the beach in the storm, drops the ramp on poor old Tony, and some big ass piece of equipment unloads, crushing all of Tony's bones, runs up the access road, hits the highway, and gone."

Carlos pointed at the laptop, "Something big enough to crush Tony would crush bushes, trees, and dig up the turf."

Steve answered, "Yes and no. The soil there is thin. It's all rock. The turf may not show it but the bushes might."

Tommy said, "Keep discussing this and make a plan. I need to take a call."

65 Calling Tommy

Cambourne
    Thursday, October 13, 2011, 6:37 AM GMT

"Tommy, our maid was killed thirty minutes ago," Alicia said starting to blubber again.

-

"Tommy, Salvatore threatened us yesterday. Shots came through our bedroom window. They killed Moira in my bedroom."

-

"We moved to an inner bedroom for protection. They killed her, Tommy. She's dead!" The tears flowed again. "This is all about the money. She's gone because of money."

-

"Tommy, just tell me what to do! I'm lost, and people are dying!"

-

"What? You'll send what over? Okay, I can wait," Alicia sniffed and gulped air. "I have to go. The police want to talk to me."

66 Unasked Question

Port Angeles, WA
Wednesday, October 12, 2011, 11:15 PM PDT

"I don't understand, Tommy. What are you asking?"

"Andy, I'm not asking for anything."

"Tommy, you pull me away for a private chat and don't have anything to tell me or ask?"

"Andy, you know what's going on. Holly can tell us what we need to know, but her price is getting out of the country illegally, which I cannot do or be a part of."

"So you want me to smuggle her out? My jet gets quarantined by customs as soon as it lands."

"I'm not asking you to do anything. You wanted to help, and you've helped already, but I have a problem I can't solve and Alicia needs help. That's all I'm saying."

67 Get in the Game

Port Angeles, WA
Wednesday, October 12, 2011, 11:30 PM PDT

"I've been giving you slack, but I need you to engage. You've been hanging back, barely speaking, and we can't afford it. I don't know what's bothering you, but I need you to get involved. Do you still want to be on this team?"

"Yes Tommy," Carmen said

"Then tell me what you can contribute. "

"I can be the contact for the marine biology prof and her students. I can coordinate Ohashi's samples with the lab."

Tommy said, "Good. What else?"

"I can work with Holly. We need detailed information from her."

"Do you see any problems working with her?"

"Yes, serious problems. If she gets out of the country we lose jurisdiction for her activities, we will have removed her incentive to help us, and given her good reason to avoid us."

"Holly is your priority. Keep her close."

68 Change of Plans

Port Angeles Police Station
   Port Angeles, WA
   Thursday, October 12, 2011, 12:30 AM PDT

Tommy gathered the team close for his orders, "Team, we need to move Holly away from here for her protection and the civilians. We have an armored SUV for the drive to Seattle. Carmen you will accompany Holly."

Nina saw Carmen glare at Tommy. Tommy did not flinch, but continued, "Andy, you and Nina can go. You should not stay here because of your association with the team."

"Steve and Carlos, you will remain here. I want you to inspect Sail River access road for recent heavy usage. The police have brought our bags from the hotel. We will not be going back. Any questions?"

69 On the Road

Washington State
Thursday, October 12, 2011, 1:40 AM PDT

Tommy sat in back next to the passenger covered with a blanket. It was getting hot under the blanket, but Tommy pushed the anonymous passenger back down as they left town. Few people saw them leave.

At Port Angeles Airport the taxi pulled up to the corporate jet. The small cab driver opened the trunk and carried the few bags up the stairs into the private jet followed by the passengers. A scruffy stranger sitting on the leather sofa stood as the passengers boarded. The cab driver removed her hooded coat and ball cap handing them to the scruffy man who put them on and left two hundred dollars richer for loaning his cab to the police.

Alan, Carmen, Nina, and Holly found seats in the darkened cabin as it pulled away from the hanger.

***

On route 101 heading toward Seattle Tommy pulled the blanket off Mark Ohashi.

Mark said, "I wonder if we fooled anyone."

Tommy said, "Carmen says they are airborne. No problems. I need to make a call. What time is it in England?"

***

On the jet Carmen asked, "How are we going to get Holly through customs?"

Holly held up her passport and said, "It should be easy. I have nothing to declare."

Carmen took it from her, inspecting it said, "This looks authentic."

"That's because it was issued by the US government."

Carmen and Andy looked at her incredulously.

"I had time," Holly said. "I got a birth certificate from a girl I met. Paid her fifty bucks. She was eighteen. I took a drivers test and got a California license. Then I applied for a passport. It cost me a hundred and twenty."

"Oh, and my name is now Diane MacIntyre, but Holly is still my nick name."

Carmen growled, "Why the big stink about getting out of the country? You could have left any time!"

Holly waved around the posh jet, "No cameras or people who want you dead."

70 Deliveries

"Tommy, thank you for calling," Alicia said.

-

"Yes, I'm pulled together now, much better. There's so much to do. I'm still in my exercise clothes. Alan took over with the police ..."

-

"You're sending a package? What do I do with it?"

-

"Okay, if you say so. That's good enough for me. Thank you, Tommy! I can't thank you enough."

-

"Yes, some debts never can be completely repaid. I'm afraid you're stuck with me."

71 Multi Level Protection

Cambourne Grounds
Thursday, October 13, 2011, 11:10 AM GMT

"Sir, there is a call. A gentleman is offering help."

"Mrs. Hodson, I am with the authorities. Please ask her Ladyship if she is available."

"Very good, Sir."

Upstairs Alicia said, " I'm still dressing, Mrs. Hodson. Ask the gentleman if it can wait."

"Ma'am, he says it is urgent. He has called on my personal cell."

"Oh, then I will take it ... This is Alicia."

"No, I will not go to the window. If you want to talk ..."

"I see. Okay, I will look."

Remembering Steve's trick, she put a hand mirror angled out toward the lake. A shaky image revealed a man standing on the lawn.

"I see you. Please come to the scullery door. I will meet you there."

Ten minutes later a knock was heard on the scullery door. The visitor heard Alicia invite him in. The first thing the visitor noticed on entering was the double barreled muzzle shoved in his face and a gruff baritone demanding, "State yer business before I air you out."

"Very good, Lady St. Claire," the Italian accent said, "I see I was correct thinking you are not a fool."

"Remove yer coat there, skippy," MacKenna demanded, "and turn around."

Salvatore complied. "It is illegal to carry weapons in this country. Of course, you are free to search me."

The Scot said, "And I reserve the right to turn you inside out."

"Let him inside, MacKenna."

Salvatore walked past MacKenna's shotgun to find Alicia pointing a pistol at him.

"Multiple levels of defense, most excellent. The very thing I am here to discuss. You understand the concept. I will help you with a bigger picture of this for you to consider."

"Come in Salvatore," Alicia said waving him into the storage room with the pistol, "Sit down in there."

72 Chatting at Gunpoint

Cambourne
Thursday, October 13, 2011, 11:20 AM GMT

"I have some recommendations, " Salvatore said, "Hide motion detectors and cameras at each door. We can install scanners inside door frames to detect weapons: metal, wood, plastic, anything. I understand you have removed electronic listening devices. Good, but not enough. Your network is compromised, internally and externally. There are listening devices outside that detect conversations inside. There could be thermal detectors. I have brought two helpers who are currently scanning the lands outside your property. After the authorities leave they will work on the grounds here."

Alicia raised the gun to eye level, "Prove to me you are not behind Moira's death."

"Certainly," Salvatore said, "I believe, like Kenneth Clark, your participation is critical to the success of your husband. Your death does not serve me in helping Cassanzos. But tell me signora, have you ever shot another human before? Do you think you can?"

"This morning I was devastated. Now, I'm mad. I will do whatever is required to protect my family. Moira was family."

73 Tanner's News

Financial District
New York, NY
Thursday, October 13, 2011, 3:35 PM EDT

"Hey Alan, how you doing"

-

"Sorry to hear dat, but I got news. Digging around some and I learned this Black Monday stock market crash a couple months back."

-

"Yeah, they're talking about bond ratings but the rumblings underneath are wondering how stable the market is. It's on account of few big players got ripped off through the system. Yeah, it's disturbing, you bet."

-

"Then you got others who are doing great. Kinda makes you wonder."

-

"I can tell ya, some big dogs are getting involved on both sides. That makes people get quiet if they know anything, ya know?"

-

"Yeah, it's all in hushed tones. No names are used, but I'll keep digging."

74 Checking In

"Ms. Ryan."

"Please, call me Sharon. Sorry to take you away from the case. I heard about the foreign actors in Port Angeles. You do seem to attract the action."

Tommy said, "Word gets around fast."

"I was talking to the tribal elders for the Makah nation. They called to say thanks and complain. Is there anything I can pass on to show progress?"

Tommy said, "Look, I'm sure you're busy. I got here late, and could use some good coffee. If you don't have time to talk now could you point me In the right direction?"

Sharon Ryan stopped and considered the FBI agent. She nodded and said, "This is Seattle. Good coffee is everywhere - except in this building. C'mon, there's a shop in the next block. I'll buy."

After settling into the window seat Sharon got to the point. "Tommy, I wanted to talk to you as a professional courtesy before getting involved with Steve Haskins."

"You're both adults. You don't need my permission, but I can tell you he is seeing someone."

"What are you talking about? Did you think ... ? Okay, maybe I worded that poorly. I mean I have a position for him, an opening, I mean work. I want him to work for us, I want to give Steve a job, that's all!"

Tommy laughed out loud and apologized, "Look Sharon, I am sorry. It's just ... never mind. I thought ..."

Sharon sat up straight and accused, "You thought I was hitting on him?"

Tommy laughed again.

"Sharon blushed, "I don't see that happening ever. I'd more likely hit on you than Steve."

Conversation halted. Tommy looked sideways at Sharon and said, "Are you hitting on me now?"

"I just said it would be more likely. Words carefully chosen. They do not constitute evidence. You can't hold me ... to that."

Tommy said, "I have it on good authority I'm not a top catch."

"Sounds like something an Ex would say. She or he is probably right, though. You're not smart, or athletic. You don't have a good job. You don't dress nice. You're not well mannered. You aren't beautiful as hell to look at, no killer smile ..."

Tommy put his hand up, "Stop, you're embarrassing me, but she probably is right."

Sharon put a white hand on Tommy's very dark hand, "I don't think you've been criticized enough. How about dinner tonight? I can tell you all the other things you're not."

"Why not? Oh, but it might be late. We're analyzing the yacht samples and autopsy results."

Sharon said, "Sounds like fascinating dinner conversation. I'm looking forward to it. This is my town. I'll make reservations for eight and pick you up in the FBI lobby at seven thirty. Don't keep a girl waiting! I have to run and you haven't touched your coffee. Oh, also, since Steve got his picture posted as an undercover cop at Occupy Wall Street there's not much future in under cover anything. I got to run. See you at seven thirty."

A few minutes later a barista set a breakfast sandwich on the table, "The lady said you have to sit here and eat this before you can leave."

Tommy laughed again and said, "If the lady said, then okay." With that he grabbed a used newspaper from the next table and leaned back.

75 Not in Seattle

Roasted Bean on Seneca Street
    Seattle, WA
    Friday, October 14, 2011, 10:10 AM PDT

"Da, he is sitting drinking coffee. I see him in window."

-

"He told woman they are testing pieces from boat. Nothing about girl. I think she is gone. Where is jet?"

-

"Good, we can finish this."

76 Date with Ms. Ryan

Metropolitan Grill
    820 2nd Ave, Seattle, WA
    Thursday, October 13, 2011 7:35 PM PDT

Sharon said, "You know, if you were in the military we couldn't date, or in banking, or a judge. You're in law enforcement, no over lap with my work. You know, you had me rattled like a school girl. I felt like I was thirteen all over again."

"If I told you I didn't enjoy it I'd be lying."

"Actually, it was refreshing, Tommy. You made me reevaluate my life. Not an easy thing to do, but we all need it, step back and look at who we are and where we're going."

"So you've chosen to become a nun?"

"Speaking of nuns, I heard the nun was with you. Wait, I don't want to go there yet. Tell me about the yacht and the giant."

"Mixing business and pleasure?"

"I like both. Why not? Tell me."

"Something hit the yacht and put a big hole in it. It should have sunk quickly but flotation bags kept it afloat. In the hold there were pieces of tube worms from the ocean floor, bits of rock and sand with muck from the bottom. No signs of anything metallic or man made."

"So was it a sea monster, or giant?"

"Forensics is still analyzing the samples and photos. Shows on TV make the forensics look so easy, but this stuff takes time."

"So, no sea serpent then."

"You're as bad as the reporters. We do have some evidence on video but there's no reason to release it and make our job any harder."

"Oh do tell!"

77 Coming Home

Cambourne
> Friday, October 14, 2011,

Andy said, "You wanted to sleep in the same room with them. Don't blame me if they kept you up. I'm not going to share a room with them. I wanted to drive out last night."

Carmen said, "You can't just barge in on people like that. A girl was killed there yesterday. We don't want to add to the confusion."

From the back seat Nina said, "You guys sound like you're already married. You sound like my parents. Why don't you just make it official!"

Carmen glared at her, then turned back to the road. Silence reigned in the front seat while Nina and Holly giggled in the back.

Two hours later the rented van drove through the village and onto the lane Tommy's instructions described. Dense woodlands enveloped them until they came through to Cambourne grounds and manor with fields flowing down to the lake beyond.

"Wow, this is beautiful! This is like a dream!"

"This is like a fairy tale!"

Andy said to Carmen, "Alicia lives here? I had no idea."

"Me neither."

Stone and red brick towered over the van as they approached the manor. Two and a half centuries ago builders determined to impress strength and nobility on all who approached. They succeeded.

At the gateway a policeman approached, "State your business here. This is an official crime scene. No pictures or autographs."

Carmen said, "We are here at Lady St. Claire's request. We have a delivery she is waiting for."

"You'll have to talk to the estate manager, and good luck. He's a hard one. I'll send him out. You wait here."

Five minutes later a big tough said, "You are here for her ladyship? Who sent you?" MacKenna noticed Carmen and said. "Wait, you, you're one of the FBI agents from New York."

"Yes, but I'm not here on official business. This is purely personal," Carmen said.

"You should a made it clear up front. Lady St. Claire could use some friends. Park just there and come through the main doors. I can give the first bit of the tour. Her ladyship would love to show you around."

Intricate carvings on the stone pillars high overhead drew Carmen and the others forward to the protective roof guarding the approach to the oak and iron doors, reminding them less of tea time and more of kings and knights defeating viking raiders, an England few outside the United Kingdom remember.

MacKenna grabbed a handle latch and pushed the massive doors open, "Welcome to Cambourne Manor, seat of Lord and Lady St. Claire."

The grand entrance and sweeping stairs took their collective breath away. The booming formal announcement forced Lord St. Claire to break off momentarily from the detective chief inspector who was interviewing Mrs. Hodson.

"MacKenna, who has arrived? Andrew Glover!"

"Alan, it is so good to see you. I didn't expect to see you so soon, but here we are."

"Yes, you are here. To what do we owe this unexpected visit?"

"Alan," Lady St. Claire said, "Who are you talking to ... Carmen!" Alicia rushed forward hugging Carmen and immediately started crying again. The desperate hug lasted until Alicia could compose herself.

"Alicia, I am so sorry, dear. Tommy just told me."

Alicia peaked over Carmen's shoulder at Andy and gave a wave. Alicia stepped back, wiped her eyes with both hands, ignoring handkerchiefs offered by MacKenna and then her husband. "Well, here we are together again heading to a funeral." She pointed at Carmen, Andy, and the girls, "This is the last time, and I mean it! Now, how are we so lucky as to get this visit?"

Carmen said, "We are here to bring you information." Carmen reached back for Holly. "This is Holly. She has information on the funds stolen from the Cassanzo family. She has come forward at great personal risk to help you recover the money."

Holly, the goth girl from Seattle, San Francisco, New York, and other places unknown, stepped forward. Alicia reached out to shake her hand, "Holly, you are a godsend. Thank you so much. We are in your debt."

"It's the least I could do since I stole it in the first place." Alicia held Holly's hand focusing squarely on her, "We are in your debt." Alicia nodded and Holly returned the nod.

Alan said, "This is a bit of an awkward time, with the shooting. I'm afraid we can't offer much for tea or lunch. By the by, where are you staying? We could put you up here ,but we are short on help and the locals are staying away."

Alicia said, "You will stay here, of course. We're all Americans, except you dear and MacKenna. I'll show you to rooms, three rooms, four rooms?"

Andy said, "Two rooms."

Carmen said, "Three rooms. I'm not spending another night with the gigglers."

Alicia led them to the stairs, "I will show you where the rooms are, linens and towels. If the beds need made we'll all help."

MacKenna said, "Your Lordship is needed with the inspector. Her Ladyship will need to sign for some deliveries as soon as she is available."

78 Deliveries

Courtyard
    Cambourne
    Friday, October 14, 2011, 11:30 AM GMT

"Three of the vans have already unloaded and left, your Ladyship. Here are the invoices that I signed for in your absence. The electronics are those boxes under the shed roof. The furniture has been moved inside, mostly filling up the housekeeping corridor. This gentleman here ..."

"Good day, Mum."

"He insists on your or his Lordship signing."

The young man said, "It's the food stuffs, Mum. I am told your credit is only good if one of you does the signing."

Alicia scanned down the pages handed to her and said, "Who told you that? MacKenna, why do we have twenty televisions?"

"Ask Salvatore about the televisions."

"The owners of the green grocer, Mum. They insisted."

"Your Ladyship, the ammunition is here, but they want cash."

"Cash? How much is it? We don't have a bank on the grounds. Tell the grocer our senior staff should be able to sign. Hey! Do not put the crates there! You're blocking the door. Where is Salvatore? He ordered most of this."

"Ah, Signora Hopkins, I have a reserve of cash for such purposes. I believe all the vans have arrived but one. Here it is now, bene, bene, the internet has arrived."

The last driver walked up, "Sorry we're later then expected. Had a bit a trouble sticking up the last mile of fiber. You did ask for us to hide it so no ugly wires about. 'At's what took the time right enough."

James Hayden, the security friend of MacKenna, stepped forward and said, "Run the fiber through the conduit just there. I'll help you test it out."

79 What are They Doing?

Tree Stand outside Cambourne Grounds
Friday, October 14, 2011, 11:40 AM GMT

"Yes Sir, there is considerable activity on the grounds. The supermarket and the green grocer sent vans over after they told us they wouldn't. A furniture van just left and there are two vans with no markings. The estate manager and the lady are haggling with the drivers. The PlusNet van we saw working down the road is pulling onto the grounds. Oh, PlusNet is TV and internet service."

-

"No Sir, we haven't seen, wait ... someone opened the door, but the PlusNet van blocked the view. I'll check the video to verify. No sightings of Salvatore or any of his crew. We did send a vehicle behind the lake to get a better view of the back of the house. Stations three, and four can see activity inside the house but it's unclear."

-

"Also Sir, there were four visitors an hour ago, two girls early twenties or younger, a man and a woman, possibly married the way they were carrying on. They went in with small luggage, and look to be staying overnight."

-

"Yes Sir, all stations have his description. We'll report as soon as he is spotted."

80 Miss Cynthis to the Rescue

Cambourne Gates
    Friday, October 14, 2011, 11:55 AM GMT

"Good afternoon Miss Strath-Whitman. It's a fine day for riding. Nice warmer weather for a change."

"Craig, nice to see young man."

"It's officer Ferguson, Mum. I'm on duty, with the shooting of Moira and all. Terrible thing that."

"Yes, very terrible, a dear child. I've come to offer condolences and any help that might be needed. There is a lot of talk going round."

"Yes Mum, you would know."

"Craig Ferguson, are you being impertinent?"

"Oh no, Mum. I only meant that people tell you everything. Only yesterday the boys were talking, 'If you want to know anything just ask Miss Cynthis, she's the one.' That's what they said, and it's true. Your sister is a bit hard to talk to, meaning no disrespect, but I can't let you by without permission Mum. Them's the orders."

"Well, I do have tarts just out of the oven. If you let me give them to Mrs. Grady I can let you have one of them."

"Oh well, I suppose if you go straight to Mrs. Grady and then out. I'm not on the Chief's good list after botching the purse snatch."

"The man ran into the wild! You couldn't have caught him with ten dogs. And I know for a fact Mrs. Sherring never carried more than ten bob on her person at any time, I don't care what she told the police and insurance men. You take this one, it's cherry and has the extra filling. Can't let anything go to waste."

"No Mum, and thank you."

"I see Mrs. Grady now at the kitchen door. I shan't be long."

"Oh, Mrs. Grady!"

***

"Best clear out, your Ladyship. Miss Cynthis is riding this way. Not sure how she got past the police. It'll be hours before she is talked out."

Alicia said thinking it through, "It's not the best time, but I did want to talk to her. Okay, invite her in, but we can't let her see what's going on. I'll keep her here. If anyone asks for me, let me know. Is the kettle on?"

***

"No, I really shouldn't stay. Poor Craig Ferguson could get in dutch for letting me by."

Alicia stepped to the door and waved to the panicking policeman wiping crumbs and jelly from his chin. Assured he had calmed down, Alicia sat with Cynthis at the sturdy table in the kitchen.

"Thank you for stopping, Miss Cynthis, and thank you for the tarts. Moira was ... there I go crying again. I'm going to be a mess for a while. I hope you don't mind having tea in the kitchen. There are a lot of police running around the house. There's so much going on and we don't have the help any more."

"Oh your Ladyship, It's terrible the things people are saying. Taylor Barnes was certain you were selling drugs, and the cobbler is telling everyone the house is haunted. The florist is afraid to deliver flowers here, but she's sorry Moira's funeral will look bare, and the air conditioner man couldn't get past the police. Bertie wouldn't help him. Clive Hayden showed him the dirt road behind the lake to get past. Bertie is so mad that he is no longer your plumber he's talking about moving away and that would be hard. He's very prompt and reasonable."

"Wait a minute, Miss Cynthis. Why is Bertie mad? He and his son are the only plumbers we hire."

"He cleared a drain for widower Simpson while telling me that's the second plumbing van coming from the manor, Anderson Brothers yesterday early and Whitman's today. He said ... "

"Miss Cynthis, I am very sorry. My husband says I am needed. Please tell Bertie we trust our pipes to no one else. Thank you for stopping by."

Cynthis awkwardly stood saying nothing watching Alicia walking away, but Alicia stopped and said, "You know Miss Cynthis, Uncle Carter was right. You are absolutely adorable."

Hands rose to her cheeks to hide the blushing. "Oh, he did not say that, did he? He's such a charmer."

Cynthis floated out and down the steps. Alan said, "Did Carter really say that?"

Alicia said, "If he didn't he is about to."

81 Mr. Harriman

Wildcat Vista Road
Snowmass Village, Colorado
Friday, October 14, 2011, 8:20 AM MDT

"Andy, is this how you show gratitude? I loaned you my jet and pilots. I offered to take you into my home, and this morning I get notified my jet is parked at London Gatwick airport. Now you're at Alicia Montgomery's house!"

-

"How I found out is not important. You have betrayed me and I won't forget or forgive! This will cost you more than you know."

-

"The jet has been recalled. You are on your own."

-

"No, I'm done talking." Click.

82 Sail River Revisited

Sail River Inlet
  State Route 112, Clallam County, WA
  Friday, October 14, 2011, 8:35 AM PDT

Steve stood on the outer beach looking up the forested slope toward the highway looking for the power line access road, so clearly seen on the satellite view. Carlos stepped through branches onto the beach waving Steve over, "You can't see it from the beach or from the road. The branches are tough. If you push into them they will swing back wide enough to get a semi through, but why here?"

"The only building here is next to the inlet. They wouldn't see the outer beach, and I believe Tony McCarty and his wife rented it. I wonder if the owners rent to anyone. Look, under the branches here, the grass and weeds grew back but the huckleberry bushes are crushed, and there too. Carlos ..."

"Yeah, I'll see if I can find the owner or a phone number. You keep looking."

Carlos circled the cove and crossed the stream back toward the suburban and rental cabin. He knocked but no one answered. He heard singing coming from a shed back in the trees. Steve followed the maintenance road up hill toward the highway. A man with a fishing pole and two healthy steelhead trout turned onto the maintenance road. Both men were awkwardly surprised.

Steve said, "I didn't know anyone was around. Are you renting the cabin?"

At that moment Carlos walked around the shed saying, "Excuse me, but ..." The man pulled a pistol and fired three shots into Carlos before Carlos fired back.

The man facing Steve dropped his gear and pulled a pistol firing once a second as he walked toward Steve who had rolled behind a stump and then scrambled backwards into the trees while drawing his weapon. Two seconds of silence and Steve rose to fire. No one was there. Steve heard crashing sounds in the woods on the far side of the road, and he pursued. More gun fire and the suburban's tires deflated and fuel poured out of several holes.

Steve dashed around the cove only to dive for cover as an assault rifle turned the vegetation around him to confetti. Loud curses seared the air followed by tires spinning in the gravel. From the escaping van Steve heard, "I will hurt you for this, blue face!"

Steve found Carlos by the shed bleeding from his shoulder and arm. Another bullet dented the center of his kevlar vest. Another man lay on his back, not moving, with eyes wide open, blood speckling his face.

Steve opened the jacket and Carlos grunted, "Vest."

"Yeah, hurts like a mother. I'll take it off after I stop the bleeding." Into his radio Steve said, "FBI agent Steve Haskins, I've got an agent down, gunshot wounds to left shoulder and right arm, critical bleeding from the shoulder. I need a life flight at Sail River inlet. He's conscious, rapid breathing. Hilo can land on the highway."

Roaring flames pulled Steve's attention away as their black suburban was engulfed. Steve jumped to his feet and drug Carlos further behind the shed. The super heated gas tank exploded sideways. Shrapnel shot past them embedding in everything upright.

83 Recap and Ready

Sail River Inlet
State Route 112, Clallam County, WA
Friday, October 14, 2011, 9:40 AM PDT

"Tommy, the hilo just lifted off. Carlos will make it. He was shot three times before his weapon discharged once. Suspect was DOG, dead on ground."

-

"I haven't been through the house yet. Bomb squad is in route."

-

"No I didn't recognize either of them. The suspect who fled had an accent, My first guess is Albanian. He threatened me . He called me blue face and ... Sandy!"

***

"I'm sorry Sir, we don't open until ten thirty," Sandy said fishing in her purse for the store keys.

The crazed man held a knife, and said, "Thees ees for my brother!"

"Wait, I have money, lots of money," Sandy squeeled as she continued fumbling in her purse. The bottom of the purse exploded and the crazed man looked at the gaping hole in his leg. He looked up in time to see the purse fire into his belt, then his chest, then his neck.

Sandy calmly picked up the keys from the ground as the man fell. She unlocked the restaurant, walked inside, and fell into a chair, sobbing.

84 Bagging the Hunter

Cambourne Basement
Friday, October 14, 2011, 3:30 PM GMT

"It's definitely a human, sir. He keeps circling that area of the meadow and into the woods, stopping every few moments," James said looking at the rack filled with monitors. "The EMF shows a human acting suspiciously."

Alan asked, "What are we looking at on the screens?"

James said, "It's the EMF detectors, Sir, electro-magnetic fields. Every living thing generates a low level field. The sensors we installed can tell the difference between a deer or a squirrel or a human. Humans show up as red dots."

MacKenna studied the movements then said, "Your Lordship, I know who that is. I'll gather him up and you can question him in the kitchen."

Fifteen minutes later the kitchen door opened and a frumpy older man carrying a cloth bag entered. "I weren't making no fuss, you need no shotgun. What's this about anyhow? A man's got a right to go for a walk."

MacKenna followed, "You've no right to be walking on someone else's property without their say so. Now sit and you'll have a cuppa tea. We'll just pretend that you have no choice in the matter."

"Well, as long as we're only pretending. Good evening your Lordship, Mrs. Grady, Mrs. Hodson."

"Freddie Barnes, what were you doing sneaking around in the woods?" Mrs. Hodson asked.

"I weren't sneaking!"

Alicia walked in and asked, "Freddie Barnes, are you any relation to Taylor Barnes?"

"Yes Mum. That's me sister."

Mrs. Grady said, "She has been saying mean things about all of us. I think she told everyone we were selling drugs. I don't think she likes us at all."

"Yup, that sounds like Taylor. It's not that she don't like you it's ... no, that's it. She don't like you. 'Specially you, Mum. Got your hooks in a rich one, Taylor says. She would'a preferred it was a local girl, of course."

Alicia said, "A local girl would have been down by ... Wait a minute, Alan was in New York. He did marry a local girl. I'm from New York, and he didn't have title, and was about to get sacked. I stayed with him through all that."

"Oh right you are, but you're not local here. You're an outsider, and American on top of that."

Alicia said, "Hmm, I see your point. MacKenna, what should we do with Freddie?"

"Freddie," MacKenna ordered, "it's time."

"Oh no, I can't. I won't do it."

MacKenna looked across the table at all present and said, "We will all have to swear never to breathe a word about what we are to see here today. This secret each of us must take to the grave. Are we agreed?"

Each in turn agreed as MacKenna looked at them. "All right Freddie, show them what's in the bag."

Freddie opened the cloth bag slowly looking around the table as if he could tell if someone was lying. His hand carefully, gently pulled out a white ball.

Silence hung until Alicia said, "It's a puff ball, a really big puff ball."

Freddie proudly said, "Giant puff balls, lycoperdon gigantea. Best mushroom there is. S'like eating steak if you cook 'em right. Jarrod

Evans give his right arm to know where I get 'em, but you're sworn to secrecy, right? And no thieving 'em either."

Alan said, "Freddie, we can't have you walking about without us knowing."

Mrs. Grady said, "Would it be okay if Freddie stopped by for a cuppa now and then. Afterward he could find his own way home?"

Freddie looked at her ladyship and nodded hopefully. Alicia agreed.

Freddie clearly relieved said, "That's a bit of all right and good thing you don't have dogs. That'd gum everything up."

Alicia said, "That reminds me, MacKenna. We need some dogs."

Freddie's face fell, but MacKenna said, "In that case Freddie, you'll have to come by more often to make friends with them."

85 Final Plans

After everyone left the kitchen Alicia said, "Mrs. Grady, we need to notify Moira's family. Do you know how to get a hold of them?"

"Your Ladyship, Moira didn't have family to speak of. We only had each other. Me, with my son and husband gone and her parents the same. She was just like a daughter, and a good one. She loved me and she worked hard. We only had each other."

"MacKenna told me you were close. I had no idea."

"No reason for you to know, Mum. We kept to ourselves mostly, 'cept when she had a beau. I protected her, but not too close. I wanted to be a grandmother some day. She was my only chance for family of my own again."

"Mrs. Grady, where do you think we should bury Moira?"

Between tears Mrs. Grady said, "She loved to walk ... by the lake ... there's the little graveyard behind the chapel there, but that's for family."

"I think it's perfect, Mrs. Grady. I'll talk to the grounds keeper."

86 News Travels Fast

Ferry to Bainbridge Island
    Friday, October 14, 2011, 11:50 AM PDT

"Steve, is the bomb squad there yet?"

-

"Port Angeles? Okay, let me know when we can get in the house. How is Sandy?"

-

"Oh, thank God. Four times? How is she holding up?"

-

"Mark and I are on the ferry to Bainbridge. We'll be there in two hours. I got a call from West Seattle General. Carlos is still in surgery. The bullet in his shoulder fragmented. He'll be okay but he's still bleeding."

-

"Yes, I called Vivian. She's flying out on the first plane. Also, we found conflicting evidence from the yacht. I can tell you more when we arrive."

87 Outside Looking Out

Outside Cambourne Proper
Friday, October 14, 2011, 8:20 PM GMT

"Rental car from airport is parked in drive, Stanis. Why do we just sit here?"

-

"The commandant is giving orders from van hidden in trees there. They have men spread all around the house but still they do nothing. Let us have phone call to make some excitement."

88 Ready, Steady, Go

Cambourne Basement
Friday, October 14, 2011, 8:25 PM GMT

As James plugged in the last of the fiber connectors to the servers and network cables to desktop computers he looked at Holly and said, "I hope you know what you're about. There's scores of people waiting on you or trying to stop you."

Holly rolled up her sleeves and flexed her fingers, "I've been doing this for a few years. I think I can handle it. Ladies and gentlemen, It's time. Connectors are good, activity lights good. We have connectivity. First things first."

The keyboard clicked furiously. First a plain white window appeared. Holly moved the mouse, clicked, and started typing again. A black window appeared with a green cursor in the upper left of the window. As Holly typed lengthy commands programs installed themselves.

"How long will this take?" Salvatore asked looking at new red lights appearing on the EMF monitors.

Holly clicked away and said, "To do things right you have to do them ... correctly. Patience is a virtue."

James' eyes widened, "PIAV, patience is a virtue! You're daemonB PIAV, the diamond bitch!"

Holly, focused on the monitor as she typed, said, "Don't call me that. I hate that name."

James pushed back in her chair telling those present, "She's the one what cracked the CeBIT security servers with all the world watching. She walked through the firewalls like they was made of paper. Wait, how old are you?"

"They made it too easy," Holly said, "There, we are now invisible."

***

Confusion reigned in a large white van on a woodman's track in the Cotswolds.

"They're gone, sir. I can see the communication to and from the house but the packets are empty. There's nothing in them."

"What do you mean? Is this a bug in their computers?"

"No sir. I can tell by the pattern they are connecting to something. The internet addresses are all over the world. This is some kind of packet encryption I've not seen before."

Sounds of a scuffle outside the van brought the doors open. Sir Smythley found a tough looking man in a blue denim jacket holding up a cell phone. "Sir Smythley, here is call for you."

"This is Smythley. Yes sir, I understand. Every cooperation, yes sir."

89 Time to Stop

Cambourne Basement
Friday, October 14, 2011, 8:40 PM GMT

Salvatore watched red dots moving all around the perimeter and said into his headset, "All points moving in. Be ready."

MacKenna said to Holly, "There's going to be a fire fight shortly. We canno' hold them out forever. Is there something you can do?"

Nina said from the back, "Wait, I can dress up like Holly and drive away."

"Very brave dear, but that won't stop them," Alicia said.

Holly said, "I still have five minutes. Carrot and stick time."

***

Smythley's cell phone rang. "Yes Sir?"

-

"It could be a ruse, Sir. All the markets will be closed in minutes."

-

"After hours trading? Very good, Sir. Standing down."

***

Alan answered his cell, but Salvatore was also listening, "This is Hopkins."

-

"We fully intend to resist your forces. Yes, but you will be a pauper long before we are dead."

-

"Yes, a Stalemate indeed. What do you propose?"

-

After a lengthy conversation Alan said, "I see. That paints an entirely different picture. I should have been told these things from the outset."

-

"Yes, your funds will be protected. No further draining of accounts? Agreed."

-

"Send funds to Smythley! What on earth for?"

-

"Very well. What do you propose for dismantling the access port?"

-

Alan continued, "The access port for stealing funds has a 'back door' I was told. Apparently the thieves were also being robbed. Stanis and his crew knew about it, but failed to inform their superiors for some reason. Self preservation, no doubt."

-

"If you don't want the authorities to learn of this access port, you must shut it down. Once the port is closed the back door will be useless."

-

"I believe you know this Stanis person, and you also know his location then. Ask him where the access port is located, or just tell him to shut it down. We will know when the port is off line."

-

"Yes, we will wait for your call."

-

"That went as well as can be expected," Alan said.

Salvatore held up his hand listening intently to his head set. "Pistol shots? How many?"

Salvatore said, "It seems Stanis was close by, but he is no longer a worry."

Salvatore turned to Holly, "Tell me about the money."

90 The Hole

Washington Marine Repair
Port Angeles, Washington
Friday, October 14, 2011, 1:25 PM PDT

The heavy duty hole saw whirred to a stop. The mechanic gave the hole he just cut and the fiberglass sawdust he had collected to Mark Ohashi.

"I'll make this official," he said loading sawdust onto a slide, "but I can see it's different."

"What does it mean?" Steve asked.

Mark said, "Just what the mechanic told us, there's no way to make a hole without a saw or explosives. One of the girls said she smelled something burning. I think they fired a torpedo made of resin just as tough as the boat with some kind of cutting edge on the point."

"But you couldn't get that kind of velocity in the water," Steve countered.

Mark said, "If the rear of the torpedo exploded when the front contacted the boat it could be enough force to lift the boat out of the water. With the big hole, it started to sink, and then the crew tripped the flotation bags and it rose back up again."

Tommy said, "It's only a theory until we get evidence. It's a good theory though. Steve, put in a call to the Navy. We need to see what's down there worth killing for."

91 Truth Will Out

Cambourne Basement
   Friday, October 14, 2011, 9:30 PM GMT

Alan explained to the small gathering in the basement,"The Lord Chancellor finally explained the trouble between Sutton and Cassanzo. The two of them cooked up an arrangement to launder money through their businesses. When Cassanzo wanted out Sutton worked the Cassanzo transactions backwards draining their accounts, the reason they needed the funds to remain in the same accounts. Hence killing the account managers was important. Sutton and some others profited greatly. The Lord Chancellor and your father did as well, Andy."

"Whatever I have that does not belong to me I want to give back," Andy said, "and I also, will return what was stolen."

Holly said, "There is a problem. I never kept records on who got what. I have lists of accounts since I started, but this has been going on for decades. I have no idea who most of the players are."

Salvatore asked, "Do you know any of them?"

"Sure, I know some."

Alan said, "Stefano Cassanzo told me two billion is what they need for a start. Holly, can you pay Cassanzos back from all the accounts?"

"Sure. I can adjust the script and automate the transactions. The only problem will be what to do with the extra money."

Alan said, "Oh yes, I was reminded Smythley will need to be paid. Apparently, Smythley lost considerable income and prestige when Sutton died. We are supposed to see that he is recompensed for lost income. Can you believe the nerve? I've a mind to leave him with nothing."

Alicia said, "Dear, do you want him as an enemy for the rest of our lives?"

Alan replied, "Buying him off will not stop him."

"Dear, you gave your word, that is the problem."

92 Seeing the Small Picture

Sail River Inlet
  State Route 112, Clallam County, WA
  Friday, October 14, 2011, 3:05 PM PDT

The captain of the bomb squad called out the door of the cabin, "All clear!"

Steve, Mark, and Tommy expected to find a frat house war zone, but the house was in military order. Even the beer in the clean fridge was in straight rows. Maps, photos, notes in Cyrillic characters. Steve studied a photo of sea stacks, rock formations off the coast and said, "This is all wrong."

Tommy looked at the notes and asked, "Steve, how is your Russian?
"

"Weak. I haven't used it in years. Gruzvik usually means truck or lorry. Povrezhden? Damaged truck, they stored the damaged truck in location number four. Sush-chest-vo? Sushchestvo."

A man at the door said, "It means creature or being." All eyes turned toward two men in street clothes walking in the door.

"Commander Louis Navato, you can call me Sonny," the leader said walking up to shake Tommy's hand. "This is Chief Petty Officer Chet McClure. Chet here is Sandy's Ex, just so we're up front."

Steve said, "McClure, I owe you a big thanks for training our girl. She spotted the mercs and took out the last one out herself."

Chet nodded toward the senior officer, "You can thank Sonny. After the last domestic violence charge he ordered me to get anger counseling and train Sandy how to use a pistol. She used a picture of me for target practice. She got way too good hitting the target."

162

"We appreciate the quick response, Commander," Tommy said, "We only put the call in an hour ago."

"Your call was not routed to us. We've been monitoring your work and your comms since you arrived in Port Angeles. Also, the merc Sandy nailed was not the last one. There are more. We aren't sure of the number."

A member of the bomb squad came out of one of the bedrooms, "Agent Edwards, you need to see this."

Tommy, Steve, Sonny, and Chet peered into the room from the hallway. Wooden crates four feet long, stacked floor to ceiling covered one wall. The opposite wall boxes marked with 'redkozemel'nyy magnit'. A crate lay open on the floor. Inside the crate were four long tubes. Rounded cones were on one end and slots along the other end. Tommy caught Chet and Sonny nodding to each other. Steve said, "Those look like javelin missiles, anti tank. The boxes are magnets. What does redkozemel'nyy mean?"

Tommy said, "Commander, what the hell is going on? There's enough missiles to start a medium sized war, and from the empty crates in the corner I'll bet some are missing. Who are they fighting?"

Steve said, I think they gave us a clue. The photo of this sea stack, sail rock? In high school we used to take boats out there to party on the flat area in the back. In this picture the flat area isn't flat. Something big is there."

93 Go Home

Carmen said, "Andy, you need to leave. You need to go home before you get hurt."

Andy did feel out of place in the middle of life and death negotiations, international money transfers but Carmen's acid tone slashed his soul. The looks from the people assembled in the basement control room echoed the insult by their lack of response. Andy walked up the steps. On the main floor he had nowhere else he belonged except his room on the second floor further isolating him.

Mrs. Hodson saw him in the hall and said, "Sir, cook has water on. You look like you could use some tea."

"Mrs. Hodson, right?"

"Right you are, Sir. The kitchen is this way."

In the kitchen Mrs. Hodson announced, "Mr. Glover would like tea before bed."

Mrs. Grady said, "I have coffee on for the others if you prefer?"

"No, tea would be fine."

Nina found Andy sitting at the large preparation table sulking over tea and cakes. "There you are! Why do you let her treat you like that?"

"She's not wrong. I don't belong."

"She was rude and you let her get away with it. You need to stand up for yourself. You act like you need her approval to be a man. You are a man, a good man with or without her approval! You also need to fire your tailor."

"I don't have a tailor."

"Right! You are your own tailor and you suck at it. I'm not talking about suits and stuff. Looks like you took your billions and cornered the market on frump. You don't need fancy shoes but they should at least be clean, and don't sleep in your clothes."

"I didn't."

Nina gave Andy the look.

"Okay, no more wrinkles."

Nina poked Andy hard, "And no more grease spots. Your shirt's dirty? Change it! This isn't for Carmen. She's mean. You should dump her. This is for you. Hold your head up. Walk around like you have value – because you do!"

Andy started smiling and Nina poked him again. "Seriously dude, you should forget about her. She treats you like shit. Don't tolerate it! Besides, a relationship is a lot more than hugging, kissing, and juicing each other up. You have to talk. You need to work on that."

Andy laid his head on the table and said, "Is she mad because she's stuck with me?"

Nina threw up her hands, "I change my mind. You are hopeless. And, it is possible she focuses on you too. Keep in mind, if she treats you like this now she'll do the same every time you disappoint her. In marriage it happens every day."

"You're right, Nina. I need new shoes. When I figure out how to get home I'll work on it."

"Yep, hopeless."

94 Confessional

Cambourne Manor
  Second Floor Corridor
  Friday, October 14, 2011, 11:55 PM GMT

"Why are you so mean to Andy. He's a nice guy."

"None of your business," Carmen said.

Nina continued, "He scares me or more like what goes on around him scares me. He terrifies the gangs, thugs, addicts ... and you."

"Shut up!"

Nina kept talking as she walked after Carmen, "He's not even my type."

Carmen said, "Nuns aren't supposed to have types."

Nina ignored the comment and said, "My dad's a cop in Queens. I've seen stuff, but Andy, he scares me."

Carmen started down the main stairs.

"You're a shrink. Yeah, he's messed up, but that's no excuse. Why are you so mean to him? Is it because he saved your life?"

Carmen froze on the landing and said "I was possessed by demons, okay?! Body, soul, and mind, I drowned in their control, in their possession, drowning in a tank of evil with no way to breathe. Yes, Andy rescued me, but in the real world he's annoying. You look for substance and there's nothing, but he's the only one I know who sees what I see. He destroyed my real world by pulling me into his."

"Maybe his is the real world and your's was fake. Either way, you can work with him without being a bitch about it. Steve's annoying. You don't treat him like that. Steve would get in your face if you tried. You can get away with it with Andy. So either you're a bully or you're in love with him and he disappoints you. Which is it?"

"Why are you with him?"

"Don't worry, Andy and I are not together. He's my guardian ... kind of, but I owe him for helping me out. You didn't answer my question and that is an answer."

95 Recalled

Cambourne Manor
    Carmen's Bedroom
    Saturday, October 15, 2011, 2:35 AM GMT

Carmen fumbled for her phone, "Hello?"

-

"Tommy, what time is it?"

-

"I'm not sure, Sir. Andy lost the jet. We'll have to fly commercial."

-

"Yes, sir, I'll get him back as quickly as possible. Understood. I'll arrange it now and text you the details. Because we aren't here on official business I can't guarantee any special treatment."

96 The Advisor

Early morning started to lighten the sky. MacKenna knocked on the open bedroom door as Andy packed, "Mr. Glover, there is a gentleman in the entrance hall asking for you. This is his card."

A few minutes later Andy walked into entrance and addressed the tall, polished young man, "Arthur Perlman is it? Can I help you?"

"Mr. Glover, I came to offer my services. I'm Aaron Fridman's nephew. We heard about your falling out with Mr. Harriman. My uncle thought you might need some assistance."

"I'm not sure how you can help. I just need to get to Seattle as quickly as possible."

Arthur said, "Mr. Harriman's jet has been recalled. There are no Gulf Stream 650's for sale anywhere, but I've made arrangements for a Gulf Stream 550. It's slightly smaller but has the same flight range. If you will authorize me, I can contact O'Bannon to put one million on deposit for a test flight to Seattle. If you like the jet I think we can get it for twenty. The flight crew is from San Diego, and they have considerable international experience."

Andy said, "I don't understand, why would you or your uncle do this?"

"Because you are going to hire me to help you get organized and on your feet. Uncle Aaron can't mentor you directly, but he can advise me and I can advise you."

"Okay, we can try this out. How soon can we leave?"

"I already have a limousine waiting. I've arranged for the rental car to be returned so you don't need to worry about it. If we leave now we

can eat on the jet. The 550 can be fueled and ready to depart as soon
as we board. I'll call ahead with the flight plan and have customs meet
us on the tarmac. I'll need the names of the passengers and passport
numbers."

"Wow, great! I'll call the ladies. The sooner we get airborne the
better. You dress very sharp. Where are you from, Arthur?"

"Sir, I'm from Milwaukee. My mother fell in love with the sharpest
dresser in town, My father is a tailor."

"That's convenient. Thank you, Arthur."

97 In Flight

The jet was smaller but had the same number of seats, less opulent, more practical. Eight of the seats could be laid flat for sleeping. Carmen sat in the back more sullen than usual. Arthur's arrival plus Nina's advice gave Andy temporary direction and potential for a future. Also, he was not sitting alone.

"No offense," Arthur said to Andy, "but Nina doesn't look like a nun."

Nina glared across the aisle, "Okay smarty Arty, what do I look like?"

Arthur met her gaze, "More like some hot military chick or maybe a cop I'd like to see on a calendar."

Nina looked stunned, then slumped back into her seat and said, "Andy, tell your butler he's sexist and I hate him."

"I'm not a butler, and my name is Arthur!"

Andy interrupted, "Arthur, I like the jet. Will you handle the sale?"

"Yes, the company won't budge on the price, but I got them to to cover a thorough cleaning and engine over haul. We should land in Port Angeles in four hours. The jet will leave for the maintenance and I'll have a chartered jet standing by. I've made reservations at the Red Lion Hotel for you and Nina, separate rooms. Do I need a room for Carmen?"

"Carmen?" No response. "She must have other plans," Andy said as he went back to reading ancient documents on line.

171

98 Other Plans

Westminster, England
Saturday, October 15, 2011, 1:30 PM GMT

"Thank you for joining us, Wynton."

Sir Smythley bowed to the seated Chancellor and nodded to the small group of power brokers. He, of course, knew the head of MI-6 and was on first name basis with the First Sea Lord, and the Chief of General Staff.

First Sea Lord began, "Smythely, we thought it best to bring you on board with a top secret project. Your assistance could prove invaluable. We are exploring the acquisition of a new kind of super stealth weapon. We need you to step in and manage the effort, boots on the ground, that sort of thing. If you are willing, we have a military flight waiting."

Sir Smythley said, "I'm your man. What type of weapon are we discussing?"

"Before we get into that," the Chancellor said, "there's a minor detail we need to discuss concerning Andrew Glover and the Hollingsworth estate."

Wynton Smythley said, "If we are opening that book again, I would like to discuss Lord St. Claire and his wife."

"Lord St. Claire is untouchable per Kenneth Clark. You had a hand in that, if you will remember."

Smythley agreed, "Yes, Chancellor, but his wife has no such standing, and you will find St. Claire more amenable in her absence."

MI-6 said, "She threatened to dent your dome with a paper weight, if I recall. It's a mistake to make this personal."

The Chancellor concluded the topic by saying, "Lord St. Claire is untouchable."

99 Environmental Changes

Port Angeles, WA
Rented Office Building
Sunday, October 16, 2011, 7:45 AM PDT

"Welcome back, Priss,"

"Did we miss anything?" Andy asked.

"It's a lot more complicated," Steve said. "At least two groups are wandering the towns and hills, heavily armed. Military is trying to keep a low profile to avoid an open firefight. SEAL teams are on the hunt. We can't use bombs or missiles so the fun is limited."

"What do they want?"

"That's just the first piece. The yacht was pierced by a mechanical object from the sea floor."

"What?""

Steve pointed to a paper and said, "It gets better. The detailed scan of the sea floor revealed a large vehicle of sorts. The Colonel here is guessing it's some kind amphibious truck."

Colonel Hawk Richardson stepped up, "It has a footprint similar to a LARC LX modified for deep sea work."

Steve continued, "Andy, this is Colonel Richardson. We have several sightings of a large crusty looking vehicle on highway 112, always late at night. We are pretty sure this is what came ashore the night of the storm and killed Tony McCarty. The Albanians staying at Sail River were obviously working with it ... if our assumptions are correct."

Carmen asked, "Then what was the thing the first boat captain saw?"

Tommy said, "And that is why I had you bring Andy back. Andy?"

Andy said, "The thing in the water had waves breaking on it. Lightning struck it. Probably not a spirit, strictly speaking. I'm researching some possibilities."

100 Unseen World

Ridge Northwest of Lake Crescent
Clallum County, WA
Monday, October 17, 2011, 3:20 AM PDT

Earlier the same morning SEAL squad Alpha Bravo watched the gap across the valley where drones earlier showed four heat signatures near the top of the ridge. Loud thumping disturbed the pre-dawn silence.

"Charlie baker, I have an audible disturbance. Request a fly over on ridge seven at previous location. Over."

Ten minutes later the SEAL's ear piece buzzed, "Showing fading heat sign at previous. Movement on far side but no heat signature. Over."

"Roger. We're moving out."

An hour later SEALs scanned the hollow from the ledge above. Thermal showed minimal sign. Night vision showed equipment, some stacked, some scattered. Chet crawled over the edge while his partner watched the perimeter through his sniper scope. In the light of dawn video of the site uploaded to the satellite.

"Two cold tangos, at least I think so. I'm looking at puddles of goo in small depressions, bones and clothing, and some equipment mixed in. Thermal registers residual heat. If this is some new kind of weapon used on 'em it didn't leave enough for an autopsy. Are you seeing this?"

-

"I have evidence bags for the goo. They also had serious ordinance up here, grenades, AR-50's spread all over, no fire, no pit."

-

"Roger, checking out the back side of the ridge."

101 Other Side

HMS Falkland Situation Room
  Canadian waters near Church Point, Vancouver Island
  Monday, October 17, 2011, 8:15 AM PDT

Sir Smythley, on board the the lead ship, fumed as he called the number. As before the call was picked up without any greeting.

Smythley said, "Just arrived. Latest contact botched. Exchange unsuccessful. Other players interfering. Delivery arrangements still in place but new drivers will be sent."

The line went dead.

"Damn! That settles it," Smythley said grabbing the Albanian by the hair jerking his head back while violently shaking the chair where he was tied. Blood and saliva flew back from the open mouth. "We gave you the magnetic nets, and you betrayed us. Who else are you dealing with? Who is out there?"

The Albanian gurgled, "none, no one."

"Two of my men were killed last night - my men! I want the weapon now! Where is it!"

102 Retirement Plans

Holly sipped tea while trying to explain illegal transaction to Alicia. The others discussed weapons around the security screens a short distance away.

Alicia pointed at the list on the screen, "So who are these people? For example, who is this?"

Holly quietly said, "Who are you looking for? Anyone special?"

Alicia said, "Someone very special."

103 Kid Gloves

"Andy, you look awful, Sandy said. "It's either existential or girl problems."

Nina said, "Existential, now there's a word you don't hear in a bar too often."

Sandy said, "So which is it tough guy?"

Andy said without looking up from the laptop, "Yes."

Sandy pulled out a chair and sat and asked, "We hear the shooting up in the hills. Are these the same guys?"

Nina said, "Hey, I thought you were off work."

"See the Jeep in the parking lot across the road? That's my Ex or a couple of his buddies armed to the teeth and guarding this building. There's another SEAL out back doing the same. This is the safest place in town."

Andy looked up from his laptop and said, "There are terrorists from several countries trying to find some weapon up there."

Nina said, "Andy is looking for the ocean going giant."

"Where do you look for information about giants?"

Andy pointed to the ancient manuscript on his laptop and replied, "In the Book of Giants, of course."

"You're funny." Turning to Nina, Sandy said, "He is kidding, right?"

Andy continued, "We only had references to the book until the Dead Sea Scrolls were found. The copies are in bad shape and most of the book was lost, but there is enough to piece together part of the story."

Nina mumbled, "At least Arty's not here to pretend he knew all this."

Andy's eyebrows went up as he looked sideways at her.

104 Redefining Impossible

Olympic National Forest
 SEAL squad Fox Delta, North of Lake Pleasant
 Monday, October 17, 2011, 10:50 AM

"Three tangos east of the rock spire.

-

"Yes, there is a rock spire. I'm looking right at it."
 Rockets ripped across the valley slamming into the spire without exploding.
 "Wait, tomahawks launched at rock. The rock is moving! I say again, the rock spire is moving west over the ridge toward Makkah Bay, I shit you not!"

-

"It's moving fast, already over the ridge. We lost sight, sir."

-

"Estimating 100, 120 feet tall. Also, missile payloads removed. Tangos are firing blanks."

***

Colonel Hawk Richardson turned to the civilians and said, "There is no heat signature on this ... thing, and it keeps knocking down our drones. Tell me what we are facing."

Tommy nodded to Andy who said, "A ton of guesses here, but the story from the pieces we have suggests this is an ancient nephilim, half angel, half human."

Hawk said, "Not a lot of time here. Talk faster!"

Andy gave a deep sigh and jumped in, "Angels or heavenly watchers came down and took wives, any wife they wanted. Their children had unusual size and abilities, the nephilim. They were extremely violent to humans. God told them in dreams to repent or he would wipe them out. They refused and good angels destroyed them and the fortresses they built. The flood of Noah was to destroy man and any nephilim remaining. Human DNA was getting mingled. Noah was perfect in his genealogy, no nephilim DNA corruption.

Apparently, there was at least one nephilim who repented. Since all air breathing life on the surface of the earth was killed in the flood, I am guessing this rock is the remains of his body after thousands of years, and his spirit is the force keeping the rock together and powering it."

"Bull shit! This is the best you have?"

Tommy said, "Andy's story fits the facts. Some rock creature living underwater, no heat signature. If he told you it was an alien, would you belive him?"

"No, but it would be easier to sell than bible stories."

Tommy asked, "Angels or aliens, it doesn't change anything. You've been turning off the hydrophones to cover for it."

105 Changing of the Guard

Cambourne Hall, Basement Control Room
Monday, October 17, 2011, 9:00 PM GMT

Lord St Claire spoke into the phone, "The presence of your forces is intolerable. They are turning back food and service deliveries. I demand their immediate withdrawal!"

Alicia said, "Tell them we want our internet service back, also."

Alan, Lord Sinclair, added, "And we'll need the internet service turned back on."

-

"Yes, immediately!"

-

Alan terminated the call, "Smythely is somewhere else. His assistant said the internet service will be turned on, but our first action must be to reimburse Smythely or the service will be turned off again and the blockade will continue."

Alicia said, "So they didn't know about our satellite connection. No problem. We have the transactions ready to repay Sir Smythely. Go ahead, Holly."

Holly nodded and her typing produced white letters on the black screen. She looked up at Alicia. Alicia nodded and Holly hit the enter key.

106 Bagged

(Conversation in Albanian)

"Fire left!"

Fiery missiles streaked through the dark mountain valley impacting without exploding in tree covered slopes. The rock figure stopped his dash up the north face of the ridge, but then continued his enormous strides up the steep incline.

"Fire left again! Hit him this time!"

Two more streaks flew, one striking the stone chest sending the dark gray thing sliding down ridge breaking massive trees in his passing. Getting his feet again, the monster dashed to the south slope.

"Fire right! We are close. Move in behind to prevent him going back.!"

Two more streaks missed but completed the objective as massive stone legs turned and ran west down the river drainage toward the bay.

As the stone man reach the beginning of the wide rocky river delta another director announced over the radio headsets, "Here he comes. Fire!"

Twin cannons fired projectiles connected by a single cable. The cable wrapped around the chest as the rare earth magnets at the ends of the cable found each other completing their unbreakable death grip, pinning upper arms to the rocky torso.

"It is holding! Fire all cannons!"

Staccato blasts sent wave after wave of metal cables weighted with heavy powerful magnets wrapping legs and arms. The figure's forward momentum continued while he lost balance sending him face first into the shallow river delta at the edge of the bay.

"We are ready. Call up the tractor."

From the dark water of the bay a massive amphibious vehicle rose from the waves, dropping a ramp on the stones. An earth mover powered up and surged forward into the initial drops of rain.

107 Climate Change

Rented Office Building
  Port Angeles, WA
  Monday, October 17, 2011, 11:15 PM PDT

"Ma'am, you can go home or back to the hotel. The threat is gone, but there's a big storm almost here."

Sandy spoke to the camo'd and armed serviceman at the protected side door, "Threat doesn't exist or it moved on?"

"Moved on, ma'am. We'll leave cover for the town, but the units are moving out."

"Go get 'em Scotty and take care of my FBI guy."

"Will do ma'am," the soldier said smiling.

Walking back to the conference room Sandy conveyed the message. Carmen sat quietly. Nina explained how everything was better in Brookline for anyone who would listen.

Mark Ohashi said to Andy reading his laptop, "At least she's not from California. That would be even more annoying."

Sandy interrupted, "Andy, I was wondering if you could walk me home. It's only three blocks."

Outside Sandy said, "Steve tells me you're a bazillionaire. So you hang out with Tommy's team for kicks?"

Rising wind blew in the first drops as Andy said, "I only got the money a couple months ago. I'm still trying to figure out what to do with it. Tommy's team are the only people who make me feel like I belong. Most of the time I feel like I belong."

"Well, I must say you're looking better and more confident, happier than when you left."

"Thanks, I had some help."

"From Nina?"

"Yeah, Nina and Arthur."

"Arty? He's your butler."

Andy said, "Nina told you that. He's not a butler. He's my assistant, and he's sensitive about his name, 'Arthur'."

Sandy continued walking and said, "So it would be inappropriate to call him Arty Farty, Mr. Fancy Pants, Arturo Juandisimo, the big butt?"

"What!? When did all this come out?"

"In the office while you were reading. Apparently, he texted her, but she never gave him her number. She was hopping mad. I'm surprised how long she carried on, and you didn't notice."

"I've got other things on my mind."

Sandy continued, "Speaking of not noticing, how about you and Carmen. She gets quiet when you are around. She doesn't talk or even look at you. Sometimes she closes her eyes."

"We were a thing for a minute, literally a couple days. Then she pulled back."

Sandy hooked her arm into Andy's arm and said, "Carmen is gorgeous. She's from New York City. You are, or were, a frumpy westerner. Maybe not someone she expected to fall for. And I must say, you are looking pretty sharp, the haircut, the boots, leather coat - pretty nice, but still not New York."

Andy smirked, "Nina cut my hair. Arthur picked out the coat. I'm just trying to focus on a bigger problem."

108 The Impossible Accomplished

HMS Falkland Situation Room
  Canadian waters near Church Point, Vancouver Island
  Tuesday, October 18, 2011, 8:15 AM PDT

Smythely snapped to attention holding the phone's handset tightly, "Yes sir, thank you sir! You should tell them yourself, sir. I'm putting you on speaker, sir."

The First Sea Lord said, "I am recommending commendations to the entire crew from a grateful nation. This technology defeats sonar, EMF, and thermal detection. Britain will once again be the leading navy in the world. Sir Smythley, as a retired commander your compensation will be fitting our extreme thanks on this risky endeavor."

Smythely said, "Speaking for Captain Hartinger, his crew, and myself, thank you, sir for the opportunity and honor you have entrusted with us."

109 Blood Money

Camborne Hall, Basement Control Room
Tuesday, October 18, 2011, 7:15 AM GMT

"Transactions are complete. Smythley is reimbursed one hundred million euros."

Alicia said, "Thank you, Holly. Please shut it down before anyone else asks us for money."

Holly shook her head, "I can't. The back door is coded onto a programmable chip on some network router."

"How can we get to it? Where is it?"

Holly said, "I thought it was at the IXP in Seattle. One side of the router is connected to Seattle, and the other side is connected to Tokyo."

Alicia asked, "IXP, what does that mean?"

"The internet exchange point, IXP, is where the undersea cables come ashore and connect to the US main internet branches. This router might be bolted on to the cable to Japan. I couldn't get past the military grade security to get into the building let alone the underground vaults where the cables join."

James Hayden walked over and said, "I overheard routers and IXP. Planning a big time hack? I'm in."

Holly said, "No hack, just trying to find a router. One side connects to Nippon Telephone in Tokyo. The other to the Seattle IXP."

James stated, "Oh that's simple. It's attached to the undersea cable between the two."

Alicia looked to Holly for explanation. Holly shook her head saying, "That's impossible. You can't open the cable underwater. It would have to be inside the IXP building."

James smiled, "I did some work in Broadway 40, biggest IXP in the world. They have tighter security than Tower of London. They scan for all routers and all addresses attached to them. Besides, there's ships to repair undersea cables. Why not hack 'em where no one can see 'em."

Alicia's eyes widened, "The FBI is investigating a deep sea attack off of Seattle!"

110 All Ashore

Submerged Freighter Irkutsk Class D-520
  US Territorial Waters
  Tuesday, October 18, 2011, 7:15 AM GMT

(Conversation in Russian, swearing in Albanian)

"No, we move slowly. If Americans find us we end up in prison."

"Captain, if sushchestvo gets loose there won't be any pieces big enough to put in cell. Avoid sharp rocks. We don't want cables damaged."

"Sharp rocks are everywhere! You added buoyancy bags to keep it off the sea floor, yes?"

"Of course captain, but currents are strong. A mistake here will be our last."

"Dimitri, calm yourself. I have hidden under their noses for two years. If the sushchestvo moves you can stun with electric."

Overhead the US spy plane scanned, constant underwater sonar pings went unanswered from sonar buoys and American submarines as the Russian made craft crawled slowly into deeper water. The storm moved in making the search for the stealth submerged craft all but impossible.

Lightning preceded the curtain of wind and rain striking rocks and waves seeking a grounding connection. The sea passively received the charges dissipating each strike. The electrical charge spread through the water until the charge was barely discernible in the ocean's myriad electrical fields. One strike filled the water around the D-520 craft until it met the submerged cargo desiring, craving, absorbing the charge from the heavens. Holes formerly holding eyes opened as the charge sucked into its being. The sushchestvo moved fingers of stone and lifted its head.

"Captain, the thing is moving!"

"Are electric cables attached? Give it shock."

Large array capacitors released a sudden jolt along the length of suschestvo causing it to jerk. A low rumble of sound rolled through the Russian ship as the creature was freed one hand. Panic shot through the crew watching through windows or on monitors.

The frantic captain turned the capacitor dial to full discharge and hit the release button. A flood of current surged. Rivulets of molten rock flowed across the creature's surface. A blast of sound preceded two stone arms bursting multiple steel cables. Massive hands grabbed the towing cables and wires pulling the ship backward. The reinforced fiber hull was no match for the angry tearing and crush. The hull, the bridge, and the hold jolted as the crew's world shook, then ripped open, then crushed like an empty beer can.

111 Go Oft Astray

Atomic Submarine USS Mako
Location Unlisted
Tuesday, October 18, 2011, 7:15 AM PDT

"We found it, sir," ensign Johnson said. "It's got a weird water distortion signature, but I can detect its movements."

Lieutenant Hardaway said, "So we can't see it if it stops. Can the spy plane see it?"

"There's an R135 overhead. Checking in with them. Gray44, can you ID the craft?"

The ensign reported, "Gray44 had a shadow tracking north around Wa-atch Point. but lost it around the sea stacks. He's dropping more sonar buoys."

The lieutenant shook his head, "Sonar doesn't work on the thing."

"It should work on their vessel, sir."

The sonar operator snapped the headphones off his head proclaiming, "Holy shit! What was that?"

Hardaway said, "I heard it through the hull! What happened?"

"Unknown, sir. A deep thrum followed by a ... a roar? Was that a roar or a crash? Gray44, did you copy?"

Lieutenant said, "Put Gray44 on speaker."

"... nothing on sonar," the metallic voice overhead began mid sentence, "but I've got a thermal plume. Spectral shows possible oil stain. Looks like you heard some bad news for your bogey. Sending coordinates for fast attack boats."

The captain entered the stations area and said, "We want the bogey but we're more interested in their cargo. It might be on the loose and moving. We need to keep it from deep water. I want a ring of depth charges to drive it ashore. Gray44, fighters are aloft. Order the strike. Let's put a warthog in the air to insure proper direction."

Turning to the comms officer captain ordered, "Raise Colonel Richardson. Give him status. Once this thing hits dirt it's his problem."

Gray44's voice came back on, "Storm's coming. Visuals will be an issue. I've got F35s loaded with jellyfish ordinance in bound, 30 seconds."

Everyone held breath.

Gray44 said, "Curtain of ordinance deployed."

Soft thumps could be heard in the sub starting slowly building in rapidity.

The captain ordered, "Gray44, I want another wave of jellyfish ready. Get them aloft. We need to keep the bad guys from deep water and the Canadian side."

Gray44 replied, "I've got a surface disturbance one click south of Cape Flattery. No thermal, no EMF signal,"

The captain looked to ensign Johnson. Johnson said, "No sonar contact. This thing is invisible."

The captain said, "Comms, tell Richardson we found the tech he's looking for."

112 On the Road Again

Rented Office Building
Port Angeles, WA
Tuesday, October 18, 2011, 7:20 AM PDT

Steve walked into the office and announced, Hi folks, pack up we are moving camp to Neah Bay. Colonel Richardson wants us close for consultation. Mark, Nina, you are staying here, you too Carmen."

Mark said, "I'm missing everything!"

"I need to go with you," Carmen said flatly.

Steve barked, "Why? All you do is mope around."

"I'm not moping."

Really, what do you call it? What is the professional term for the long face and not talking to anyone even when they're talking to you?"

Carmen looked at him intently, then looked around the room and said, "I'm listening."

Steve snarled, "Listening to what?"

Carmen looked around at Mark and Nina staring at her. Even Andy, who had returned, lifted his head out of the laptop. Carmen said, "I'm hearing a voice or voices."

Steve laughed harshly, but Andy asked, "What are they saying?"

Carmen shook her head and said, "It's not words, more like emotions and images, thought images. If there are words, I'm not hearing them."

Steve threw up his hands, "Oh great! Now there's two flakes to deal with."

Andy asked again, "What are you hearing or feeling?"

Carmen's eye's widened and mouth hung open. Then she said, "Frustration before but now sudden fury like I have never known. Now it's more like an evil satisfaction. It's far off, but clear, and it's coming from this direction." Carmen pointed to the west.

Andy said, "Steve, we need Carmen with us."

"Well, that's where we are headed. Gear up. We're moving out."

113 High Cost of Innovation

Forward Mobile Operations Unit
Bayview Road, Neah Bay, WA
Tuesday, October 18, 2011, 8:55 AM GMT

Before dashing out of the Explorer into driving rain Andy asked, "How is it you hear this voice?"

Carmen said, "How do you not hear it? It screams at me. I think it is from one person or thing. I'm trying to differentiate the streams of thought and feeling, but they are all jumbled up."

"We need to move people!" Steve demanded. "Colonel Richardson does not like to be kept waiting."

"Wait! Before we go in there, Carmen, is it possible your connection to this thing is two way? Can you communicate to it?"

"How?"

Andy said, "Try thinking of your strong emotions or thoughts. See if there is any change in the stream you are receiving. Can you affect the stream?"

Steve said, "Time to go kids. Talk about it inside."

Hoods up and a mad dash to the soldier holding the door of the communications trailer put the team into the control of a lieutenant who herded them left into a waiting area next to a tribal elder wearing a Red Sox ball cap, "The Colonel will call for you when he needs you. Until then stay behind the lines on the floor and keep conversation to a whisper."

Steve and Tommy stood with the Colonel.

114 Do Your Part

Camborne Hall, Main Entrance Portico
Tuesday, October 18, 2011, 5:10 PM GMT

The gentleman with umbrella deployed walked the hundred yards from the gate to the main entrance portico through the misty rain.

"That's far enough there, Skippy. State yer business!" McKenna barked from behind the shotgun.

"My business is with Lord St Claire, you ruffian," the gentleman said with a slight quaver.

"I am here, Bagley. What do you want?"

Alicia loudly demanded, "Is that Smythley's assistant? Let me hold the rifle."

"Not now, love," Alan said over his shoulder.

Bagley stated, "Sir Smythley, if you please." Then to Alan he said, "Lord Duffington, the First Lord of the Admiralty requires you to immediately contact your former charge, Andrew Glover, and request a meeting."

Salvatore whispered to Alan, "Keep him talking. Find out what he wants."

Alan spoke out the window from behind the stacked sand bags, "Why should I help. You have been nothing but a menace to my home and family."

"Because this is why Mr. Clarke put you in this position. If you show good faith all watch on your properties will be withdrawn."

"What am I supposed to discuss with him?"

Bagley said, "Tell him of your current predicament, and request his help."

"So, in other words, you don't care about the conversation. You only want to establish his location."

Alicia spoke low to Salvatore and Alan, "Smythley's been paid. Why do they need more help?"

115 Missing Pieces

Port Angeles, WA
   Tuesday, October 18, 2011, 9:15 AM PDT

Andy's cell vibrated. Alan Hopkins's name appeared on the screen. Andy whispered into the phone, "Alan, I can't talk much. What's going on?"

"Andy, it's Alicia. Two things. First, Smythely is probably close by and is looking for you. I'm sorry, but this phone call is for locating you. Second, we think there's an undersea cable near Seattle that's been compromised. Basically, it's been breached, and used for stealing money from Cassanzo's and others. Can you get this to Tommy?"

Andy replied, "He's twenty feet away. I'll tell him."

116 Gone to Ground

Cape Flattery, WA
Tuesday, October 18, 2011, 9:17 AM PDT

A second string of jellyfish ordinance detonated in a moving curtain of deafening thunder and shock through the water off shore from the Fuca Pillar sea stacks, pillars of rock remnants, ghosts of an older shore line. The surface disturbance half in and out of crashing waves crawled further toward cliffs towering above the surf.

In the mobile command center, in the back corner, behind the painted line for observers Carmen fell to her knees. Andy saw her go down, but his attention was pulled toward the communications officer informing, "Jellyfish deployed. Target moving to shore. Spec Ops moving in, sea and land."

Colonel Richardson opened his chirping cell and listened before finally saying, "Understood. We have captured materials we can use."

Tommy saw the Colonel's hand move to his side arm and then away before he ended with, "Richardson clear."

Richardson turned to the command and control team, "Bring up the magnet cables. We can't kill this thing, but we can wear it down. It has limited energy. Then tie it up and haul it out."

Andy knelt down with Carmen and whispered, "Is he hurt or afraid?"

Carmen eyes flared. She spoke through clenched teeth. This thing has no fear. It is angry and drawing its enemies into a trap. It's done this before ..." Carmen gulped, eyes growing wider and she completed her sentence, "over thousands of years! There are images of huge numbers of giant attackers this thing has survived. We are nothing to it."

Carmen shook her head and said, "Wait, you said 'He.' You know who or what this is!"

Andy said, "I told you I had a guess. You just confirmed it. This is bad."

"You need to warn the Colonel."

Andy stood. He called out, "Colonel, this is a trap. That thing is drawing you into a trap."

The lieutenant guarding the door declared, "Silence until you are called on, or you will be removed!"

The Colonel said, "How do you know this?"

Andy pointed to Carmen, "She is sensing its emotions and mental images."

The Colonel turned to Tommy, "How trustworthy is this information?"

Tommy stated, "I have confidence in my team, but the information is tough to sort out at times."

Andy spoke over the lieutenant's hard stare, "There's more. An undersea cable was breached, the nephilim is drawing you into a trap, and Smythley is here looking for me."

Steve turned hard and marched toward Andy. Through clenched teeth he hissed, "Priss, tell me you picked out your heirs!"

"I was working on it until I ran into Nina and then ..."

"You had one job, only one! You've put us all at risk again trying to protect your ass again!"

117 Disaster Calling

Camborne Hall, Scullery Door
Tuesday, October 18, 2011, 5:25 PM GMT

Alicia stepped to the kitchen door, "Stephen, I told your son any of the senior staff are authorized to sign for deliveries."

"I know mum, but Marissa heard from Addyson Strath-Clyde, she's Miss Cynthis' sister ..."

"Stephen, I know who Addyson is."

"Yes mum, but she heard from her cousin in London your accounts was bare. Marissa says if you sign yourself then you might have a pity on us common folk when the few bills do get paid."

Alicia bit her lip smiling at the absurdity of moving hundreds of millions around the world, but now the green grocer at the back door feared not getting paid.

The camouflaged man in the tree stand some distance from the front gate viewing the exchange through binoculars entered the phone number in the cell phone. As soon as he saw Alicia sign the receipt he hit send.

Stephen snapped the metal clipboard with a loud pop. Alicia jumped.

"You seem a bit jumpy miss."

Alicia gave a worried smile and said, "I'm sorry Stephen. There's been a lot of worries since Moira's death."

"Yes, mum."

In the tree stand the man redialed and hit send while Alicia and Stephen chatted about poor Moira. Alicia closed the kitchen door as the man furiously hit send a third time. The van turned around in the courtyard and headed for the gate while the unseen man descended.

***

In the basement security area, James turned to Salvatore, "Sensors outside the front gate picked up a cell signal close by while her ladyship talked to the green grocer. The signal dampener stopped any incoming."

"I will need the sending and receiving numbers." Then to his cell phone Salvatore said, "Niccolo, I need the green grocers white van and the window lucite we discussed."

118 Closing In

Port Angeles, WA
Tuesday, October 18, 2011, 11:10 AM PDT

"Sir, the target moved to shore but we lost visual."

Colonel Richardson said, "What is the forecast?"

"Rain is thinning but a second band is expected."

The colonel called to the visitor area, "Pete Sandro, where can a hundred foot tall rock creature hide on the cape?"

The Red Sox ball cap hung up his cell phone and said, "It could pretend to be a sea stack. There are a couple caves on the point that might work."

"Get maps of the sea stacks to fast attack boats."

Steve added, "You'll need pictures too. The thing could stand next to a real one."

Richardson asked, "Pete, how many caves?"

"Maybe two deep enough. Hard to know. Waves shoot straight into the opening. We have a couple rescues every year with people trying to get boats in. It's illegal, but they still try. Don't think anyone ever made it all the way to the back. People died trying."

119 Target Cornered

Cape Flattery, WA
Tuesday, October 18, 2011, 11:35 AM PDT

Rapid assault zodiacs brought two seal squads through the rock pillars to patrol outside the cave openings, while four black wet suits fast rappelled down the face of the cliff. The first two repellers went left and right of the cave opening training weapons into the opening for cross fire coverage. A third dropped and stopped waiting for the next wave. He body surfed into the opening. Once inside the cave mouth, he fired an impact anchor into the rock wall and pulled himself to a ledge, fighting through the next wave as he lifted himself out of the churning water. Four ballistic anchor bolts attached a cable firmly to the stone.

"Anchor is good. Reel it in and join the party."

The line went taut and another black clad soldier slid down the line, curving toward the anchor, dropping onto the rock shelf.

"Alpha squad proceeding. The rest of you sissies can handle the luggage. No bogies yet."

***

Inside the comms trailer in the parking lot of the trailhead the SEAL commander and the Colonel watched video from body cams as the soldiers advanced slowly along the left hand ledge, weapons drawn, heads on a swivel. A sudden cry and a glimpse of falling rocks filled the screen. One camera showed dark, the other static.

Commander Sonny Navajo called, "Alpha report!" One heartbeat later Sonny said, "Beta, go!"

Another soldier slid down the wire and unclipped. "Wire clear." Another descended.

"No sign of alpha. Proceeding," was heard in the comms trailer. Two more body cams came on line. One minute later the lead body cam showed a rock with a gun strap hooked on it half in the water, but most of the gun was missing.

Commander Navato called, "Beta, withdraw to cave mouth." Then to Colonel Richardson he demanded, "What the hell is this? I'm not risking any more men on your experimental crap!"

"You have your orders, Commander."

"Screw orders! What are my men facing? Exactly what, none of your Joint Chiefs bullshit!"

"Potentially a non-terrestrial. It's a life form with technology to defeat sonar, thermal, even motion."

"It's not technology," came from across the trailer. Both men turned to the visitors to see Andy facing them.

Richardson ordered, "Captain, remove them!"

"Belay that order!" Navato countered, then turned to Richardson, "Before you sacrifice any more of my men I want to know what they are facing."

"It's a nephilim, sir," Andy said.

120 Disaster Response

On the other side of the world, the white trailer in the back lot of the road maintenance reserve was quiet on the outside belying the storm within. Several antennae brought waves of verbal assaults for failure to close the case.

"We followed orders. The technicians rigged the van as directed. What more can we do?"

"I was woken from a perfectly blissful sleep to Admiralty's sound thrashing and disapproval," Smythley barked through the line from the ship laying off Vancouver Island. "I ordered a thorough going over of equipment before being deployed. Obviously, this was overlooked!"

"On the contrary, Sir Smythley, we followed your directions to the letter," Niles Bagley said.

A technician in the trailer volunteered, "We can dismantle the device and review the connections."

Bagley said, "How is that possible?"

"I picked up the van as directed. It's parked outside."

"Noooo ..."

***

Bagley's exclamation of disbelief was the last sound Smythley heard before the line went dead. The last sound the road crews heard was the bone jarring eruption removing the green grocer van and the white trailer from existence. Large earthmovers blocked the maintenance office from serious damage.

208

***

Smythley, anticipating an investigation causing him more problems, placed a call to an unlisted number in London.

Police provided details to the press regarding the unsafe storage of petrol at the road department. No one carried the contradictions of the Chief engineer for roads.

At Cambourne Manor Lord St. Claire's anger roiled, "We will not be party to murder! All this must stop immediately!"

Salvatore stated, "I apologize for nothing. They attacked us. I responded with their own devices. Any investigation will point back to them. And by the way, their immediate target seems to be your wife. We are installing clear window covers to protect against snipers. They also prevent drafts as an added value. All delivery vehicles will be received at the gate here forward."

121 Misdirection or Redirection

Flattery Point , WA
Monday, October 18, 2011, 11:10 AM PDT

"It's a nephilim, sir," Andy said. "It's not an extraterrestrial. It's an extra-dimensional."

"Soldiers lives are on the line, Mr. Glover. How can we defeat it or negotiate with it?"

Andy said, "You aren't equipped to deal with it. If you sealed the cave you would not kill it, and it would get out eventually. I think I might be able to help."

Navato said, "I need to find two men missing in the cave. What can you do? Can you communicate with this thing?"

Carmen who was now seated in a desk chair looking dazed, lifted her chin mumbling, "He is waiting for you, waiting."

"What did she say?" Richardson asked.

"The nephilim is a warrior," Andy said, "from a race that ended thousands of years ago, his family and friends only vague memories to him. He is waiting for your next move.I think I can help find your men."

"Out of the question," Richardson barked. "Captain, remove them! All non military personnel leave now!"

Steve rose and led them to the door pulling on his rain slicker. Tommy and the others filed to the door. Steve raced to the suburban opening the door for Tommy as the wind hammered rain into them. Pete Sandro, Carmen, Andy, and Steve clambered in shutting out the fury of the storm.

"What were you thinking? Steve said to Andy. "Those are active duty SEALS getting destroyed down there. Warren's not here to protect you. What can you do?"

Andy smiled and said, "I didn't know you cared."

"Not about you Priss. If a civilian gets killed the paperwork never ends."

Tommy added, "This is a military operation. I have no pull, no jurisdiction. You'll need Colonel Richardson's approval to do anything."

Pete Sandro spoke up, "I believe I can help. I know a lady with a lot of pull in DC. Tommy, if you could ask her for help ..."

Tommy held up a hand and said, "If you mean Sharon Ryan, it will mean more if you call her. You're the Makah elder."

122 Tea for Cynthis

Cambourn Manor, Morning Room
Monday, October 15, 2011, 11:10 AM PDT

"Just terrible news. Edward is sure he will be investigated, and his loss of the van, well that will hurt business certainly."

Alicia sipped tea then said, "Cynthis, please tell Edward we have a new van coming he may borrow at no cost." A side look at Holly and Holly excused herself and headed to the dungeon. The dungeon, her name for the security station in the basement.

"And, if it's not an imposition," Alicia added, "could you ask Freddy Barnes to stop by when he has a moment."

Cynthis set her cup down and said, When he has a moment? The man is a perfect lay about."

"Well, at least he is good at something," Alan added eavesdropping as he walked through the morning room.

Alicia added, "And tell him that his sister Taylor is also invited."

"That will get some tongues wagging." Mrs. Hodson said.

"I doubt she will come. She has been quite negative on your marriage and setting up here in the manor."

"Tell her she will be able to see all the changes we have made. That will give her more to talk about."

Cynthis said, "I see the constables are on to other crimes."

"Yes, it almost starts to feel normal. We miss Moira terribly."

"Maybe we should not discuss her," Mrs. Hodson said.

Alicia dabbed at her eyes saying, "It helps me to talk about her, to remember her. She said the silliest things constantly."

Mrs. Hodson sniffed, "Yes, she was inappropriate at most times."

"I know our American sensibilities are difficult for you to understand, Mrs. Hodson, but I have to celebrate the common people and their brilliance."

Mrs. Hodson made no comment so Alicia added, " I also appreciate the British stateliness you bring to our lives, Mrs. Hodson. Please don't stop reminding us of our places."

Breaking the momentary awkwardness, Cynthis said, "Moira certainly made for interesting discussions in the village."

Alicia held tissue to her face and Mrs. Hodson said, "Do you remember the time Moira bought all the purple candies and ..."

123 Lighting the Fuse

Seattle Campaign Office of Norm Dicks
Monday, October 15, 2011, 11:10 AM PDT

"Sharon! Line four."

"One minute," Sharon yelled across the room.

Finishing two conversations and jotting notes Sharon lifted the phone holding it to her ear with her shoulder she declared, "Sharon Ryan."

-

"Hello Pete. I need to schedule a presser with you and Norm. Can you dress up like last time?"

-

"Wait, repeat that."

-

Sharon's eyes widened and then narrowed, "Oh, the hell you say! Norm and I will make some calls. This is going to end now, promise!"

-

"You're welcome. Can I call you back at this ..."

"Call Tommy Edwards? The FBI Tommy Edwards? That would be my pleasure."

124 Fish or Cut Bait

Flattery Point Parking Lot, WA
Monday, October 15, 2011, 11:10 AM PDT

"Yes sir, immediately."

Richardson ended the call and announced, "This operation is terminated. We will be clear of all tribal lands by 10:00 PM today."

Commander Sonny Navato growled, "We're not leaving with my men still down there!"

"I have my orders, and I follow orders, Navato. Your superiors have the same orders. Do what you want, but the resources of this joint operation are pulling out starting now."

***

In the Suburban Tommy heard pounding on the window. The rear door opened and Sonny Navato jumped in the last bench seat.

"I don't know how this unit works, but I need help getting my men out of the cave." Turning to Andy Sonny said, "What can you do?"

Andy in the middle bench looked at Tommy then said, "With Carmen's help I think I can communicate with the creature."

"How's does that help?" Sonny drilled. "My men are hurt, disabled, or dead. What can you do?"

"I can't tell you. If I tell you it won't work. I'll need to be in the cave."

Sonny looked askance and then to Tommy.

Steve said, "He is crazy but not suicidal."

Tommy added, "We have a history and a trust in Mr. Glover. If he thinks he can get in and out of there alive, I'm inclined to believe him."

Sonny nodded and said, "We only have a couple hours before we need to pull out. Meet me out on the point in fifteen minutes. We will rope you into the cave."

Andy said, "I'll need comm gear for Carmen, Steve, and me."

Sonny agreed and ran out into the rain.

Tommy asked, "Andy, I'm assuming you are sure about this."

"Pretty sure."

Steve said, "You're not sure all. You're just guessing!"

125 Boots on the Ground

Cape Flattery, WA
Monday, October 15, 2011, 11:10 AM PDT

The storm front flowed off the Kamchatka peninsula and across the northern Pacific pushing cold rain sideways in gale swept blankets as Steve yelled into Andy's ear, "You don't have to do this."

Andy faced Steve calmly, the blast shaking everything around except his resolve.

Steve nodded and shouted, "Okay, the SEALs will talk you down. When you get in the cave, it's tall but narrow. Looks like it gets wider in the back. There's a ledge you will land on." Steve reached under his rain slicker and clicked the button on his radio. "Radio check."

Andy said, "This is Priss number one, copy?"

Steve's big grin couldn't cover his concern. "I got you Priss number one. Please approach the cliff."

"Carmen?"

"I'm here Andy," was heard in the ear piece, "but what do I do?"

"Just think loud thoughts."

Andy nodded to Steve and hooked to the climbing line, leaned back over crashing waves eighty feet below, the harness pulling at his waist and legs. Once over the side the wind pushed him wildly around and he struggled to maintain his footing on the cliff side.

Andy heard in his helmet's headset, "Mr. Glover, keep breathing. Breathe slowly. Take the second carabiner and hook onto the guide wire. That will slide you down into the cave. We'll be right outside if you need us. When you find the team members attach one of the extra lines to their harness. Tell us the color of the line and we'll talk you through the rest."

Black wetsuits clipped into the rock face gave him the thumbs up. Andy forced his stressed breathing to slow down. Then he saw the camouflage fabric washing in and out of the cave on the waves.

Andy's boots touched rock as a wave washed over the ledge. He leaned forward grabbing at the cable anchor.

Andy heard in his ear, "Tide is rising Mr. Glover. The ledge will be under water in sixty minutes."

Andy said, "Carmen, are you still there?"

126 Birds on the Pitch

Canadian Territorial Waters off Vancouver Island
Monday, October 15, 2011, 11:10 AM PDT

"Video fragments show that the cables are still wrapped around the majority of the torso and legs. It is hampered, but still formidable," sounded over the speaker in the situation room where the operations crew assembled.

Smythley repeated, "But the US military is withdrawing. Did they give a reason?"

"An investigation was threatened, and an American civilian volunteered to retrieve fallen SEALs."

Smythley smiled asking, "Would that be Andrew Glover?"

"Yes, the cables still attached will slowly drain any electrical charge from the creature, and will shield it from further external charges."

"So," Smythley continued, "We will track it and capture the creature as soon as it gets into deep water after it crushes Mr. Glover, two birds in one operation."

"Do not fail us, Sir Smythley. Your team in England has suffered a setback. We need you back in England to take charge and complete the previous task with subtlety."

"Understood."

127 A Bird in the Hand

Cape Flattery, WA
Monday, October 15, 2011, 11:10 AM PDT

Andy slid one foot at a time on the wet rock ledge leaning back against the rough cave wall, the smell of spent ammunition mixed with seaweed and tidal creatures heightened the bizarre nature of Andy's already dark world.

One slow step.

A slide step.

A cautious step over a piece of metal.

Light from the cave opening faded with each advance into darkness. A sound caught his ear between waves flowing in and washing back out. Andy stopped. A human voice, no question, faint but it drew him forward. Andy flicked on his headlamp. SEALs may need to be stealthy, but Andy needed to not trip and end up bodysurfing further in. There it was again.

Andy said, "Carmen, what do you sense?"

"There are thoughts, picture of a little bird stepping into a snare."

"Great! Let me know when he's about to strike."

Faintly, Andy heard Steve curse in his headset. "Steve, mute yourself!"

No response meant he complied.

The sound was close. Well into the darkness thoughts of spiders and creepy things were held at bay until a touch on Andy's shoulder freaked him! Andy ducked and turned to see an arm reaching out from a crevice above his head.

"Andy, duck!" Carmen screamed in his headset.

Andy screamed back, "Azazel!"

Silence followed his exclamation. Finally Carmen said, "There's confusion mixed with anger. The anger is building. Watch out!"

"Shemiziad!" Andy replied, followed by, "Shemizia!"

"Andy, there is more confusion."

Andy said, "Ahlya."

Andy then he clearly heard above him, "Help."

Carmen said, "Sadness, profound sadness. There's regret he cannot cry."

Andy looked up and saw the stub of a leg hanging out further down, jagged bone dripped blood. Andy removed battery pack and radio on his belt, then wound the belt around the end of the fleshy part of the leg, pulling it tight before threading the buckle closed.

Andy spoke into the black, "Ohya. Ohya," as he worked.

Carmen said, "I see pictures of two brothers in the arms of a ghastly father hugging them."

Andy scanned around with his headlamp. The rock he stood on showed metal straps reaching up, disappearing into folds of the stone. There were devices attached to a few. The strapping wrapped around parts of the soldier.

"Steve, I found one of the SEALs. I need a battery powered angle grinder to free him."

A voice broke in, "The grinder is sliding down the guide wire. Do you need help?"

"No, let's keep it simple."

"Affirmative. Extra blades and wrench are in the bag."

Andy retrieved the equipment from the mouth of the cave. When Andy cut through a third cable, the rock ledge holding the SEAL moved allowing the soldier to slide down to Andy's feet. Andy suddenly recognized fingers in the rock shape. Looking farther into the cave he saw an expressionless face in the rock looking back at him. He realized he was standing on the Inside of a leg. Andy felt overwhelmed by the sadness and loneliness this being surely felt.

Looking down, the face of Chet McClure showed exhaustion and pain. Andy laid out the harness and rolled Chet into it. Attaching one of the extra cables trailing him, Andy said, "Green cable is ready for retrieval."

The line went taut while Andy lifted his end hoisting Chet out of the cave, and finally, up the cliff face.

Andy returned picking up the grinder he went further in cutting every strap and cable he could find.

Carmen spoke, "Andy, he is flooded by regret and gratitude for fresh memories you brought up, and for your help."

"Carmen, think about the joy I feel to help him."

Working back from where Chet was found, roughly the nephilim's hand, Andy continued cutting cables and bands he found while looking for the other SEAL.

The ledge ran out up ahead when Carmen said, "Andy, you won't find the other soldier and the tide is rising."

128 What Really Happened

The last fifty feet of the cave Andy hustled toward the anchor bolts as waves washed up to his knees. Once on top of the cliff he accepted a blanket from a soldier. The rain and wind thinned to a steady blow as Andy climbed into the middle seat of the suburban. The operations trailer pulled out while Andy was in the cave.

"Okay Priss, how did you pull that off?" Steve asked.

Andy said shakily, "Any hot coffee?"

Sonny Navato said, "Let's get somewhere more secure before we debrief. Let's meet back at the Warm House Restaurant. We can get coffee there."

Andy visibly shook on the drive over the hills back to Neah Bay. Carmen sitting next to him reached her hand over to steady him and he started crying.

Navato looked back at Carmen and said, "It's nerves. Some people throw up."

The Warm House lived up to it's name. A comforting blanket of heat surrounded them. Andy continued to shake, barely getting cup to his lip without spilling.

"There were two brothers," Andy started with, "who had dreams. The dreams were different but had the same theme. I'll spare you the details. God was going to destroy all the nephilim if they didn't stop killing the humans and some other twisted stuff they were doing. Anyway, The nephilim decided to fight God. I think there was some kind of war. The copies of the Book of Giants we have are pretty damaged, but you can make out pieces of the story."

Andy sipped coffee and continued, "Nephilim were the only life form I knew big enough to do what we were seeing, but they were destroyed in the war and then the flood of Noah."

Tommy asked, "So the Book of Giants told you how to talk to them?"

Steve jumped in, "Why the hell didn't you tell us what you were planning?"

Andy said, "Because Carmen had a connection somehow."

Carmen sighed and said, "He was only one of the voices, but he was the strongest."

Andy said, "I needed surprise. I figured anything Carmen knew the nephilim would know. And Tommy, I don't know his language. All I could find were the names of his grandfather and father. I guessed from the book this was Ohya. Ohya had a stronger fear or sorrow when telling his dream."

"So you bet your life on an old book you can't even read," Steve said.

Sonny said, "It probably saved your life. There's a lot I can't say but Colonel Richardson was compromised. We knew early on he was listening to someone other than his chain of command. Some intercepted messages suggested Andy here, was a target. They backed off when he volunteered to go over the side. When Andy exited the cave we caught several signals suggesting assets were en route or maybe already here.

129 Back to Real Life

The Gastropub
Port Angeles, WA
Monday, October 15, 2011, 11:10 AM PDT

"There's my guy," Sandy said walking forward with arms stretched toward Steve as the group walked into the gastropub. The owner directed the others to a large corner table.

Mark Ohashi said, "I don't get it. How did a crusty old guy like Steve land a babe like Sandy? She's a ten and he's, he's just a mess."

Tommy pulled out a chair and said, "He landed her because she's smart."

Nina walked in followed by Arthur saying, "My family would disown me if I brought you home. If you ever show up on 32nd avenue my father will beat your ass!"

"Nice mouth for a nun," Mark said.

"1122 32nd Avenue," Arthur said.

"2211!" Nina snarled. "You keep all these details in your head and can't remember one single number!"

Arthur said, "You confuse me."

Andy added, "Yeah, I'm confused too."

"But you got the giant, right?" Ohashi asked.

Tommy said, "Nope, the giant got away. But Andy had a chat with him first."

"What did he say? What did he sound like? What language did he speak?"

Carmen said, "Slow down Mark. First, Andy did all the talking. The giant perceived Andy as his equal."

Many eyes turned to Carmen in surprise, including Andy's.

Carmen said, "What? He knew the giant's name. He knew his family. All of you would act the same if you ran into someone who knew your father, your family. It establishes a connection. Andy had no weapon or intent to harm, and he knew the nephilim's family ... at least their names."

Sonny Navato asked, "What will the giant, nephilim, do now?"

Carmen said, "I can't sense him.

130 Calling Big Brother

Tommy said, "Her name is Sharon. You'll meet her at Thanksgiving. We're coming to your place if the invitation is still open."

-

"We're still working out the details. She has condos in Seattle and Virginia.

131 Carved in Stone

St. Clement's Chapel
Cambourne Proper
November 22, 2011, 10:10 AM GMT

The stone reminder of the life that had been Moira Reagan read, "Loving daughter, faithful servant, friend to all," followed by the dates of her arrival and passing from this world.

Alicia, Mrs. Hodson, and Mrs. Grady stood arm in arm in arm in the cold drizzle as workmen put tools back in the truck. The same size and color as the ancient headstones, in amongst the many no longer legible from weather and wear.

Mrs. Hodson said, "It would be nice to have a small bench set up under the chestnut tree, just there." All agreed without words.

Mrs. Grady held out her free arm toward Holly hanging back from the ladies.

"Come on then dearie. You belong here same as any."

Holly stepped up and Mrs. Grady looped her arm around Holly. Feeling Holly's reticence, Mrs. Grady squeezed her more and said, "You're feeling cold now but pot's on the boil and we'll be having a cuppa in no time."

Holly leaned into the cook and said, "That sounds great. Thank you. I wish I had met Moira."

Mrs. Hodson said, "Linger in the kitchen, dear. Mrs. Grady will tell you all her Moira stories over and over. In a few years you'll believe she was an old friend."

"Years?"

Alicia spoke first, "Don't think you are going any where else, Holly. You are welcome here as long as you want."

Mrs. Grady said, "We're not exactly family, but we'll grow on you, dearie. More like a good sweater, less like mold."

132 Retirement Funds

St. Jerome Manor
  Outside Geneva Switzerland
  November 22, 2011, 10:10 AM GMT

Gentlemen in business suits left the palatial mountainside residence and drove down the mountain disappearing in multiple directions. The service staff found Sir Smythley and his wife along with two security guards. The night guards shot cleanly, died quickly. The occupants of the grand bedroom appeared to have taken some time and considerable effort to achieve death. A cryptic note was found by the investigators warning of similar actions for any more theft of funds.

Notifying the British consulate started a chain of frantic communications through official channels, then back channels, terminating in an angry, anxious call to Lord St. Claire.

Alan immediately opened the secure line to Salvatore.

"This was your work, Salvatore! You will stop immediately, and address this crime!"

"I assure you Lord St. Claire, I had nothing to do with this. Despite what the note said, the Cassanzo family is quite satisfied with the monies returned to them, and I am enjoying their generosity. Could it be that missing funds from some unsavory character or group were traced to Sir Smythley's accounts?"

A thought flashed though Alan's mind. He turned to see his wife looking at him. A stunned husband asked, "Did you know this would happen? He was tortured before they drained his accounts. Are you party to his death?"

"Dear, he tried to kill us several times. He threatened to come after us again. I was protecting our family."

"But a savage response like this cannot be condoned. I ..."

"Alan dear, I'm pregnant."

-

At a lakeside villa north of Rome, Salvatore looked at his phone with raised eyebrows. Then he smiled ending the call and returned to his lovely companion's conversation.

The End

About the Author

The author, K N Boyle, comes from an Irish American family of storytellers. Using his exposure to business, ranching, surfing, accounting, farming, engineering, religions, computers and IT, he weaves the facets of life into relatable stories of everyday people in extraordinary times.